Somewhere a
Pebbles clatter

Tessa McAllister reined ~~~~~~~~~ stop, settling him with a calming hand at his neck. He blew hard through his nostrils, his muscles tense as he danced sideways on the narrow trail.

Early evening was prime time for wildlife activity, and there could be anything lurking just out of sight. Whatever it was, Dusty wanted no part of it. And with loose rock on the trail and a thousand-foot drop only inches away, backing up would be a dangerous option.

"Easy, Dusty," Tessa murmured, reaching down to unbuckle the strap on her rifle scabbard.

A deafening crack split the air—then something slammed into her thigh with searing force. She caught just a glimpse of a dark pickup truck rocketing down the lane. Stunned, feeling strangely disoriented, Tessa reached down to touch her scuffed leather chaps, then stared.

Her hand was covered with blood.

Books by Roxanne Rustand

Love Inspired Suspense

*Hard Evidence #81
*Vendetta #87
*Wildfire #91

*Snow Canyon Ranch

ROXANNE RUSTAND,

an award-winning author of seventeen books, is truly delighted to have this opportunity to write for Steeple Hill's Love Inspired Suspense line.

Her first manuscript won a Romance Writers of America Golden Heart Award for Best Long Contemporary of 1995. She was a *Romantic Times BOOKreviews* Career Achievement Award nominee in 2005 and won the magazine's award for Best Superromance of 2006. She has presented workshops at writers' conferences from coast to coast, and she is a member of the American Christian Fiction Writers Association, the Faith, Hope and Love Chapter of RWA, Authors Guild and Novelists Inc.

Roxanne and her husband live on an acreage in the Midwest and have three children, two semiretired horses, a couple of goofy border collies named Elmo and Harold and a number of very demanding cats. She loves to hear from readers and can be reached through www.shoutlife.com/roxannerustand and www.roxannerustand.com, or by snail mail at Box 2550, Cedar Rapids, Iowa 52406.

WILDFIRE

ROXANNE RUSTAND

Steeple
Hill®

Published by Steeple Hill Books™

STEEPLE HILL BOOKS

Steeple
Hill®

ISBN-13: 978-0-373-44281-2
ISBN-10:   0-373-44281-5

WILDFIRE

God's mercy is so abundant, and His love for us so great, that while we were spiritually dead in our disobedience He brought us to life with Christ.
—*Ephesians* 2:4–5

Many, many thanks to Lyn Cote, for her support, advice and friendship. You are such a blessing in my life!

Heartfelt thanks to my husband and children, whose patience and understanding have helped me pursue my dreams…and to my dear mother, Arline, who encouraged those dreams from the very beginning.

And as always, to Johanna Raisanen and Krista Stroever, the wonderful editors who made this series possible!

ACKNOWLEDGMENTS

Many thanks to Brian Rustand, whose love of fly-fishing, high adventure sports and the Tetons provided me with wonderful research material. Thanks also to Wally Lind, Senior Crime Scene Analyst (retired), and Phyllis Middleton, for invaluable information on fingerprints and crime scene assessment. Any errors are entirely my own. Continuing thanks to Lyn Cote, Diane Palmer, Pam Nissen and Jacquie Greenfield. And finally, thanks to author Jennifer AlLee, who helped me find the perfect name for the injured dog in this story!

ONE

Somewhere ahead, a branch rustled. Pebbles clattered down a rocky slope.

Tessa McAllister reined her horse to a stop, settling him with a calming hand at his neck. He blew hard through his nostrils, his muscles tense as he edged sideways on the narrow trail.

Around the next bend, she remembered, the path widened as it crossed a lane leading to an isolated cabin, then it disappeared into a heavy stand of pines. Early evening was prime time for wildlife activity, and there could be anything lurking just out of sight.

A mountain lion.

A mama bear and cubs.

A moose protecting her calf—aggressive and more unpredictable than a bear, though at least it wouldn't eat people.

Whatever it was, Dusty wanted no part of it. And with loose rock on the trail and a thousand-foot drop only inches away, backing up would be a dangerous option.

"Easy, babe," she murmured, reaching down to unbuckle the strap on her rifle scabbard.

He threw his head and fought the bit, flecks of foamy saliva flying, his tail lashing in agitation as he danced in place.

It was likely that the "predator" ahead was on two feet instead of four—though even the human kind could be dangerous, given the recent rash of thefts in the area.

But growing up on a ranch in the Wyoming Rockies had prepared Tessa to defend her life and livestock at a moment's notice. And whatever loomed ahead, it was blocking the only way down this side of the mountain.

She waited a good five minutes, and when nothing scary came around the bend, she urged Dusty forward, singing, "Oh, Susannah" at the top of her lungs to warn away any wildlife.

The gelding's ears flicked back and forth as he shook his head.

"Everyone's a critic," she muttered as she stood in the stirrups for a better view.

Now, she could see the dense stand of brush flanking the road. The birds abruptly fell silent. She felt Dusty's back tense. She urged him forward, one halting step at a time.

A hint of silver glittered through the bushes.

Someone uttered a harsh curse.

A deafening crack split the air—then something slammed into her thigh with searing force.

A heartbeat later, she glimpsed a dark pickup rocketing down the lane ahead. Stunned, feeling strangely disoriented, Tessa reached down to touch her scuffed leather chaps, then stared.

Her hand was covered with blood.

Sitting on an exam table at the tiny Wolf Creek Medical Clinic, Tessa silently berated herself for taking this trip into town.

Clouds of billowing dust had marked the fast retreat of that mysterious vehicle as it tore away. Surely the shooting was an accident—a stray bullet during target practice, maybe, or someone shooting game out of season. Either way, if the guy realized what he'd done, it would account for his panicked departure.

But with those unanswered questions, the fact that she and Gus were in town—leaving no one to watch over the ranch—filled her with unease. Even his wife Sofia, who was the cook and housekeeper, was away.

"I could've treated this wound myself," Tessa mumbled, watching Mary Andrews, a physician's assistant, finish cleaning her wound. "It's just a scratch."

"No, your hired hand was right. This needed to be taken care of here." Mary looked up at her and smiled. "I suppose you would've used your cattle salve and antibiotics?"

"Right." Tessa gritted her teeth against the pain. "I—I've patched myself up before."

"Not a good idea. I've *seen* the handiwork of some of the cowboys who've come in after they've gotten an infection or haven't healed right. Anyway, you were due for a tetanus booster." Mary leaned closer and inspected the three-inch furrow gouged across Tessa's thigh. "You're lucky. A few inches difference, and it could have hit a major vein or shattered your femur. How on earth did this happen?"

"Accident." Tessa shrugged.

But what if it wasn't?

She'd urged Dusty into high gear to put distance between herself and any further danger, then a mile down the trail she'd had to pull him to a halt while she stopped the bleeding. As the initial numbness wore off, the pain had steadily increased, and it had been a long, difficult trip back home.

Mary laid out a tray of dressing materials and tore open a packet of sterile gauze squares. "After I finish this, I'll give you a tetanus booster and an injection of long-acting antibiotic. I'm also sending you home with an antibiotic prescription. Make sure you finish the bottle, okay?"

Tessa nodded. Earlier, she'd been preoccupied with making it back to the ranch. Putting her horse away. Staggering to the house, all the while trying to hold her makeshift bandage in place.

Now, in the quiet of the clinic, the memory of that unexpected gunfire made her shiver.

Her eyes warm and compassionate, Mary seemed to read Tessa's mind. "A delayed reaction, I'll bet. Happens all the time after accidents and such. Can I give you an extra blanket while I do this?"

Tessa drew in a steadying breath, and managed an answering smile. "The sheet's fine."

Bells chimed over the front door, then the sound of male voices drifted down the hall. Tessa could hear her hired hand Gus, who was waiting in the reception area, plus a voice she didn't recognize.

"The clinic is closed, so that's probably the deputy." Mary tipped her head. "Want to talk to him while I do your dressing?"

Tessa glanced at the clock. "It would save time. Gus and I need to get back to the ranch."

Mary called out, and a serious-looking young deputy, with Gary Hayes on his name plate, appeared at the door, a clipboard in hand. He stood there, uncertain, a rosy blush staining his fair cheeks, even though Tessa was well covered by her shirt and a hospital drape over her hips and legs.

"The sheriff is busy," he said. "He'll stop by your place as soon as he can. In the meantime, I need to take your statement."

Tessa winced as Mary started applying the dressing. "I was on the trail that skirts the Chatsworth cabin. Maybe six or six-thirty."

"Did you see anyone at all in the area?"

"Nope."

"But when you called 911, you said there was a vehicle."

"I'm pretty sure it was a pickup. The road from the main highway up to that cabin is washed out in a couple places, so I doubt anyone could've navigated it in a car."

"Color?"

"Dark—that's all I know. I caught a flash of something shiny—probably a bumper—but the vehicle was obscured by brush, and then it left in a hurry. I couldn't guess at the make, model or exact color."

"Do you think the driver figured you'd seen him? Panicked, maybe, over leaving a witness?"

"A *witness?*"

Looking up from his clipboard, Deputy Hayes fiddled with his pen as Mary finished applying the dressing to Tessa's wound and administered the two vaccinations.

"I'll go to the front office and write up my progress notes," Mary said to Tessa, giving the deputy a pointed glance. "You two can just come on out when you're done talking."

As soon as she left, the deputy's mouth flattened to a grim line. "Your brother-in-law couldn't be here right now, because he's investigating a crime scene at the cabin."

Tessa stared at him. "W-was someone injured?"

"The owner lives in Denver, and this is his luxury weekend hideaway. He wasn't there, luckily. From what we can gather after talking to him on the phone, there was at least a ten-thousand dollar loss from theft and vandalism."

"Any clues?"

"I don't know yet. But you might've stumbled across our suspects, and they could be afraid you can identify them." The deputy slowly shook his head. "So if I were you, Ms. McAllister, I'd watch my back."

* * *

Josh Bryant stepped off of his vintage Harley Electra Glide and lifted off his helmet. He ran his fingers through his hair, then unzipped his black and white leather jacket and took a good look at the dusty, sleepy two-block stretch of businesses.

The faded sign on the edge of town read Wolf Creek, Wyoming, Population 986. From the appearance of the boarded-up buildings on the outskirts, the town had faced serious problems through the years.

Here, though, there was growth—a coffee shop, a couple of antique shops. A store offering gifts and flowers. A tiny office advertising Tourist Information and Chamber of Commerce in its dusty storefront window, and a few other shops farther down. Evidence that the town was probably gearing up to attract the rising influx of vacationers and wealthy land buyers from out of state.

He'd heard about the area from his old girlfriend Tessa, during their freshman year of college. Before he accepted this assignment, he'd done some online research and learned that a number of McAllisters still lived in the area...including Tessa's mother, Claire, who owned Snow Canyon Ranch. Through the wonders of the Internet, he'd also discovered that Tessa seemed to be running a wilderness outfitting business at the ranch, though maybe she simply owned it and lived elsewhere.

Given her aspirations back in college, he hadn't expected to find her in Wyoming at all. And given her bitter, final words to him years ago, he doubted that she'd be very welcoming. Still, a local contact would be helpful—especially if the ranchers found out why he was there.

Though Tessa didn't know it yet, she could be his ticket to freedom from a life of more pain, heartbreak and overwhelming guilt than he'd ever thought possible.

And the sooner he got this project done, the faster he could leave.

At the tiny Chamber of Commerce, Josh found a Snow Canyon Outfitters brochure with directions to the ranch and a phone number. It also showed a map of the general area of the mountains covered by Tessa's outfitting company. Numerous trails crossed the western boundary of the ranch and snaked up into the high country, then fanned out over a vast area where customers could opt for scenic rides, fishing, or hunting expeditions.

After calling the ranch and reaching someone who said Tessa would be returning from a pack trip this afternoon, he'd gone out to set up his campsite, then started out on foot carrying a backpack filled with camera equipment.

With luck, his GPS system and that map, he might be able to intersect the pack trip on its way back. He'd have the elements of surprise and innate Western hospitality on his side. She might even be happy to see him. With another casual encounter or two, he might be able to convince her that despite their past, they could be friends.

It was a perfect plan…

Until he heard the steady clopping of hooves and caught sight of her leading a string of six horses and riders down from the mountain, and every last part of that plan crumbled to dust.

"Aren't we back yet?" The nasal voice piped up from the middle of the pack for the third time in ten minutes. "This trip was way too long!"

Tessa swiveled in her saddle, one palm on her gelding's hindquarters, the other pressing against the still-painful muscles in her thigh. This group of six had opted for an easy, one-night trip, meant for photographing scenery and wildlife, but the night had been too cold and the day overcast.

Growing up with a hard, no-nonsense mother like Claire, Tessa had little tolerance for whiners and complainers, and this group had both in spades. "We're nearly at the ranch border. After that, we're less than an hour from the home place."

"An hour!" One of the men groaned and stood in his stirrups. "Would've been better off on foot. I told you girls that. But, oooooh, no. *We* had to rent *horses*."

The "girls," all at least in their fifties, nodded in agreement, their heads swiveling as one toward the imperious, silver-haired matron on the last horse in the line.

Dusty jerked to a halt, his head up, his ears pricked.

Tessa whipped around to face forward, a dozen dangerous scenarios flashing through her thoughts. Rifle fire. The panic that would ensue amongst these soft city folk if they had to make a fast escape. They'd probably all fall off in the dirt if their horses broke into a lope.

Dusty's head bobbed up and down, as if trying to focus on something.

And sure enough, someone was crouched in the shadows, still as granite, facing the side of the path maybe a dozen yards ahead. Intently looking at something…or was he *waiting* for her to draw near?

Her pulse stumbled at the thought of how truly vulnerable she and her customers were.

He slowly straightened. Turned. Reached up and twisted the bill of his ball cap from his nape to front—and then she saw what he held. A camera, with a long telephoto lens.

Relief melted her muscles to jelly as she sagged in her saddle. "Howdy," she called out. "Just passing through."

He nodded, stepped farther away from the trail to let them pass.

But at the moment she looked over to smile her thanks, her heart lodged in her throat.

She stared at his tall, muscular build.

At his face—so different now, yet still the same; its lines and planes sharper, more defined. The jaw line more resolute.

But there was no mistaking those blue eyes or the deep waves in his black hair…even if his eyes held shadows and secrets that hadn't been there before.

Josh.

The shock on her face surely matched his.

He'd walked away from her ten years ago, leaving her with the most devastating situation of her life. Damaged her faith. Changed the course of everything she'd dreamed of while growing up on her mother's ranch.

And he was most definitely a man she'd never, ever wanted to see again.

TWO

From the expression on her face, he was the last person she'd ever hoped to see.

But with that long, strawberry blond hair and those pretty green eyes, he could have picked Tessa McAllister from a crowd of thousands. Stunned, Josh stared at her in disbelief as a hundred images from the past rushed through his thoughts. He'd decided to arrange a casual first meeting, hoping it would help him ease the two of them into a comfortable friendship.

He hadn't counted on the impact it would make on his heart.

She'd been strong. Stubborn. A petite gal with big dreams and the determination to make them happen, and he'd fallen in love from the moment they met. They'd broken up after a stormy fight by late winter and he hadn't seen her since, but it took him years to get over her. Even now, her name brought back the poignant memories that he'd tried so hard to forget.

"I thought I recognized your voice," he said finally,

taking in her sun-browned skin and her well-worn leather gloves. Her dusty chaps. The lariat on her saddle.

Everything about her appearance indicated that she was back to ranching full-time, and he was surprised at that, because she'd been so determined to go into medicine. Why hadn't she followed her dreams?

"I...can't believe it's you, way out here." Her smile was faint at best. "After what—ten, eleven years?"

"Ma'am, can we keep going? I can't stand this saddle much longer!" One of her customers called out.

"And my wife and I have dinner reservations," her husband added. "Let's go!"

She raised a hand in acknowledgment, her eyes never leaving Josh's face. "We're just a few miles from my mother's ranch. Why are you out here?"

"I work out East, but always wanted to cross the USA on my old Harley. Same one I had in college," he added with a smile. "Remember? Black, with all the chrome and a red leather seat."

She barely nodded.

"And I finally had a good excuse to make the trip. I'm out here on a photo shoot."

Most people were fascinated by his job and promptly peppered him with questions. Tessa's shoulder lifted in an almost imperceptible shrug.

"Have at it then," she said, making a beckoning motion to the riders following her. She touched the brim of her Stetson hat and nodded as she passed by.

It had been stupid, coming out here to seek out

Tessa as an ally. Thinking he could shelve his old emotions easily as a stack of old and inconsequential photographs.

Because just as before, he felt a flicker of his old, soul-deep attraction to her.

And all he really needed was to be alone.

During the following week, Tessa led several overnight pack trips—a group of teachers who came out for a weekend under the stars, then three fly fishermen looking for cutthroat trout up in the higher elevations, where the spring run-off hadn't turned the water brown with silt.

Today, she'd gone out alone to check cattle, and things hadn't been good.

Gus hobbled out of the main horse barn when she dismounted. "Find the cattle?"

"I found thirty head loose, about a mile northwest of the summer pasture. The fence was down." Tessa hauled the saddle and blanket from her gelding's back and settled them on the hitching rail, then took off her gloves and slapped them against her chaps to shake off the dust. "Ten are missing."

He tipped the brim of his hat up with a forefinger. "What did they do, just plow through it?"

"Nope. The fence posts were upright, but it looked like the barb wire was cut."

"Figured there was trouble, just from the look on your face. I know for a fact that those fences were solid just a few weeks ago."

Gus had ridden up there alone, something that had worried her from the moment he left until the minute he returned to the ranch, but she'd been busy with calving, foaling and customers who had flown in from Oklahoma, and she'd had no choice but to let him go. *Someone* had to ride fence on the summer range before they drove cattle up there, and it should have been Ray, her much younger hired hand.

But Ray had abruptly quit the week before, and there'd been no answers to her advertisement in the local paper. None from the job listing on the ranch's Web site.

Today's disappearance of ten valuable cows was just one more aggravation added to many—and would mean days of searching for them. Meetings with the sheriff. Endless rounds of phone calls and faxes to sales barns in a four state area.

But it wasn't only the fence and missing cattle that were bothering her. Gus had been more like a protective uncle than an employee, since her childhood. There was no sense in getting him riled up at hearing that Josh Bryant was in the area. With luck, Josh was already on his way out of Wyoming, and wouldn't be back.

"It's only May 15th," she said. "Seems too early to be having much trouble with campers, and I don't think anyone else is starting pack trips up into the high country until the end of next week. Too much snow."

"You think it's them thieves that were over at the

Langley ranch?" Gus scratched his jaw. "Five, maybe six head of their black baldies disappeared."

"I'll call Michael." She untied Dusty and led him over to the pasture gate a few yards away. "There's a definite advantage to having a brother-in-law who's a sheriff."

Gus nodded. "Good man."

And he was right. Michael had been a homicide detective before accepting a job as acting sheriff last year, and had won a special election held in January, when the former sheriff decided to retire due to poor health. He'd certainly brought big-city skills and ideas to this county, something that had been long overdue.

When he and Tessa's sister Janna married last month, they'd invited the entire town, and the crowd had nearly overwhelmed the Community Church where most of the McAllisters had attended for generations.

Claire hadn't gone in years, just on stubborn principle.

Tessa hadn't been much better.

She gathered up her saddle, bridle and saddle blanket, and lugged them into the tack room just inside the barn. After so many hours in the saddle, her wounded leg ached and she had to concentrate to hide her limp from Gus's concerned eyes.

But when she came outside he was still standing there, with his arms folded and a flinty expression on his face.

"It ain't safe, you going up in the hills alone. Especially when you're hurt. Shoulda had me come along," he said.

"I needed you here while I was gone, Gus. I can't let some little accident change how I live my life."

"That wasn't no 'accident,' missy," he retorted.

"There's no reason for anyone to take a potshot at me," she said firmly. Their eyes met, and she knew he was thinking the same thing she was—maybe she didn't *personally* have any enemies, but there were plenty of people in the county who had good reason to resent her family. "Anyone call about my ad in the paper?"

He shook his head. "Nope. And my Sofia just told me that Danny still hasn't called."

Tessa felt her stomach tense at her housekeeper's message. "He was supposed to stop out on Monday, but he didn't. I left two messages on his cell phone and e-mailed him last night."

Gus snorted in disgust. "You've given that boy too many chances already. He runs with a bad crowd, Tess. What happens if he starts drinking on a pack trip?"

Danny Watkins had worked for her during the past two seasons—ever since Tessa had started her Snow Canyon Ranch Outfitters company. He was just twenty-three years old, but had grown up in the area and was already a highly skilled fishing and hunting guide; personable and charming and responsible...so far.

But he'd also been in some serious legal difficulty as a teenager, and somewhere along the line, he'd fallen into trouble with alcohol. Last winter he'd been in a fight at a party and had been arrested.

"He needs this job. The tip money is far more than he could ever make in town, and he's saving for college." She bit her lower lip. "He's never brought any alcohol on a trip. Not once. He *promised* me he wouldn't."

Gus snorted. "That's what he says. But a promise ain't going to hold water if he really feels the need, Tess. You know that."

She did. And yet…"I just need to give him a chance. If we cut him loose, what will he do? What kind of job could he find around here? I've told him he'll be fired instantly if there's ever even a hint of trouble. He understands that."

"Maybe that's why he ain't calling you back."

"Then I guess the decision was his. I'm just trying to be forgiving, Gus."

He gave her a long, knowing look, as if he could see straight into her heart. "Too many people want to judge others, and it's a hurtful thing. You've been on the wrong end of that too many times. Just don't go too far in the other direction. He could do something stupid and cause a lot of harm."

She watched Gus shuffle back into the barn, then she turned toward the house.

She knew all too well about judgmental folks in this town; the ones who resented her mother and who took pleasure at any opportunity to see Claire McAllister or her daughters stumble. Tessa had always done her best to ignore their whispers and lies and sidelong glances, but she'd still had a place at her mother's ranch, and a blanket of security.

Danny had nothing—his dad was gone, his mom was disabled. He needed someone to give him a break, and she was going to give him every chance she could...though there were folks in town who didn't feel the same.

There'd been another break-in at a remote cabin owned by wealthy, out-of-state people. Someone had hauled away thousands of dollars worth of fancy electronics, fine art and expensive fly fishing gear.

It had to be someone who knew the backcountry, because no one had found so much as a clue about the perpetrator's identity.

So...just how well did she know Danny and his rowdy friends, and how far could she trust them?

THREE

Danny didn't call, but he did show up the following week, saying he'd lost his cell phone and hadn't checked e-mail lately, because he'd gone north to hike Mount Moran.

Tessa breathed a sigh of relief when he pulled up by the barns and stepped out of his old '87 Ford pickup with an easy smile on his face. Tall and lean, with the wiry build of a long-distance runner, he looked as if he hadn't eaten in days, and as always, her first impulse was to invite him in for one of Sofia's wonderful Mexican meals in an effort to fatten him up.

"Supper?" She smiled, anticipating his answer.

His eyes closed in an expression of sheer bliss. "Is Sofia still here?"

"She and Gus have been here since before I was born, and I hope they'll stay the rest of their lives. Supper ought to be ready in just a few minutes, so let's head on up to the house."

Danny fell in step with her. "I heard you got shot. You okay?"

"Just a scratch—some fool target practicing, I suppose. No big deal."

He angled a doubtful glance at her leg, clearly noticing her slight limp. "Gonna be up for any pack trips or trail groups this summer?"

"Absolutely."

"How's the schedule so far? Got many reservations?"

"It's always light the first few weeks of the season. But you can still start the end of next week, right? I've got a party of four scheduled for a pack trip up into the high country starting Thursday and coming back Sunday."

Danny's eyes gleamed with anticipation. "Fishermen, right?"

"You got it. With the spring run-off, the water's too cloudy downstream, but it's crystal clear up in the high mountains. I'm thinking the confluence of streams below Reacher's Canyon ought to be nice. The snow has melted at that altitude."

He nodded. "Are we dropping these guys off? Or do they want a guide?"

"Guide. I'll help you pack them up there, then I'll meet you on Sunday afternoon to help you bring them back down." She smiled. "These four are flying in from New York, so if all goes well you'll probably earn some nice tips."

He beamed at her. "Awesome!"

"We need to talk, though, just so there aren't any misunderstandings later."

They walked up the steps of the big wraparound porch, where she ushered him through the main entrance and past the spacious living room, to the main floor bedroom that she'd converted into an office. She waved him toward a chair, then settled behind her desk and pulled out two copies of an employment contract. She handed him one.

"Same as last year. Starting date is May 21 which is next Wednesday, through November 1. Same rules— absolutely no alcohol, drugs or cigarettes at any time, whether on Snow Canyon Ranch property or up in the high country. No rough language, either. People spend a lot of money to come out here for the fresh air and clean, beautiful environment. Understood?"

He ducked his head. "You almost make that sound like an accusation."

"I had nothing but compliments about you last year, believe me. Clients said you were a great guide, and many said they'd never been on a better pack trip." She smiled warmly at him. "I just figured we should start out on the right foot."

With his red hair and freckles, his fair skin had always betrayed his emotions all too easily. Now, a bright flush worked up the back of his neck. "You heard about last winter. About that party."

She met his eyes. "Yes, Danny. I did."

His gaze veered away. "I might have run with the wrong crowd in high school, but that isn't who I am now. I want to make something of myself, and that one night in January was just a big mistake. Wrong people, wrong place, wrong time. It won't happen again." A corner of his mouth lifted in a rueful smile. "I suppose you heard about it from your brother-in-law."

"It's public knowledge. It made that little court reports section in our newspaper. I just wanted to make sure that you and I were square about expectations."

He thrust out his right hand and gave hers a firm shake. "We are."

Sofia peered around the corner of the open office door and rapped softly on the frame. Her eyes lit up when she saw Danny. "I was hoping you'd join us tonight. Gus isn't in yet, but supper's on the table so we'd best get started."

Danny followed Sofia and Tessa to the dining room, and took his usual seat. "The tourists are starting early," he remarked after Sofia gave the table prayer. "And crazy as ever, it looks like."

Tessa rolled her eyes. "I can hardly wait for the real influx—bumper to bumper cars heading north. Crazy city drivers. Bear and moose jams on the highway if just one of those people think they see wildlife."

"It's started already." Danny accepted a platter of fragrant enchiladas from Sofia, helped himself to one, and passed them to Tessa. "There was sure one crazy driver up on Highway 49. I saw skid marks, and it looked like he was going too fast and missed the sharp curve. He must've laid his motorcycle on its side before going over the edge, 'cause there was a fender up in the middle of the highway."

Tessa felt her heart skip a beat. Tourist season

wouldn't be in full swing for another three or four weeks, and there was little traffic—mostly just local ranch trucks—on these remote roads. "A *motorcycle?* What kind?"

"Harley, I think."

"What did the bike look like?" she asked sharply.

A forkful of enchilada halfway to his mouth, Danny looked at her in surprise. "Big and black, with a red leather seat and lots of fancy chrome." His voice turned wistful. "Can you imagine going cross-country on one of those things?"

Tessa's fork clattered to her plate. "Did you see *any* sign of the owner?"

"Nope." He shrugged. "I stood at the top of the cliff and looked, thinking I'd see a body, but there wasn't anyone down there. I think the rider must've bailed out before the bike went over the edge."

"You didn't go down to look?"

"Believe me, I had a clear view. Anyway, you'd need a good fifty-foot of rope to get there."

Tessa pushed her chair away from the table and stood, her uneasiness growing. Josh had said he was still riding the cycle he'd had in college. It fit Danny's description.

But no matter who that motorcycle belonged to, nighttime temperatures hovered close to freezing, and if he was still out there, hurt and confused, wandering in the opposite direction of the highway could be a fatal mistake.

"I'll be back in an hour," she called over her

shoulder as she ran for her truck keys. "I'll eat when I get back."

"I'm coming, too," Danny said. A dull red flush crept up the back of his neck, and he angled an apologetic glance at Sofia. "Sorry—but she might need some help."

On her way out the door, Tessa flipped open her cell phone and called the sheriff's department to see if there'd been any ambulance or wrecker calls for a motorcycle accident on Highway 49.

None—which sent her at a run toward the barn for some rope.

The dispatcher promised to send out a deputy to check on the situation, but there was no time to lose. The scent of blood could lure predators from miles around. An aggressive bear had been reported in the area.

And with so few deputies to cover the entire county, help could arrive too late.

Pain knifed up Josh's left leg as he struggled to his feet one more time. Blinding, searing pain that sent his stomach roiling with nausea and made black spots dance in front of his eyes.

The last thing he could remember was coming into a curve and discovering a moose standing in the middle of the road.

Sometime later—was it minutes? Hours? He'd opened his eyes to see a nearly vertical cliff rising above him, a good thirty feet of rocky outcroppings and heavy, almost impenetrable brush.

God had been with him during the crash, because the Harley must've gone airborne to have made it past that rugged terrain, and he'd landed in heavy brush that had slowed his fall. When he'd finally managed to lever himself up enough to look around, he saw the crumpled machine was a good twenty feet away.

He'd applied a pressure bandage to a deep laceration on his lower leg with his shirt, but it had bled through in no time and had slipped off twice. The leg itself was fractured, he had no doubt about that.

And calling out for help had been futile. During the hours since the accident he'd heard only a couple of cars go by, and this early in the year there wouldn't be hikers out on the trails. No one would think to look down here.

Thirsty beyond bearing, he'd fashioned a make-shift splint out of a Wall Street Journal and a couple of shirts that he'd managed to pull out of the saddle bags on the bike, then he'd tried to follow the distant sound of a stream. He'd alternately crawled and staggered, leaning on a long branch he found nearby, the pain escalating as the swelling increased in his leg.

He'd finally dropped to the ground, exhausted, which made him guess that his time on earth could be limited. He could deal with the laceration. He could re-bind his makeshift splint. But the dull ache in his side was growing, which could be an indicator of internal injuries. If that was the case, struggling to reach safety could just exacerbate any bleeding.

And not one person knew where he was.

The irony bit deep. For the past year, he'd wanted nothing more than solitude. He'd rejected the concern and hovering of his mother and two sisters. Turned away friends. And now, only his editor knew that he was in the Wyoming Rockies, but she certainly didn't know what part—much less that he'd been on this particular isolated road.

He looked around, the edges of his vision dimming as another excruciating wave of pain rolled through his belly.

This was a beautiful place. Soaring pines. Cool, crisp mountain air. Through the trees to the west, he could see the first streaks of an amber and rose sunset. Of all the places he'd ever been, this would be the most beautiful place to die, surrounded by God's glory.

Funny, how after turning away from his faith since after Lara's death, that he still felt a sense of peace and acceptance and comfort enfold him now…

As if God were welcoming him home.

He hitched himself back so he could lean against a rock, and folded his arms around his midsection.

And then he bowed his head in prayer.

"It was here," Danny said. "I'm sure of it. Let me out."

The highway was narrow and curvy, bordered by

steep, granite cliffs on the left and precipitous drop-offs on the right; the shoulder offering just scant inches of gravel between asphalt and air.

Tessa stopped and let him climb out of her truck, then drove ahead slowly, frantically searching for a place where she could pull off the road. She finally found a safe spot a quarter mile past the curve and slammed on the brakes.

Leaving the emergency flashers on, she clipped a can of bear repellent spray to her belt, grabbed a lariat and her rifle, and ran back to Danny.

Her pulse raced as memories of Josh crowded through her thoughts, coupled with a burning sense of guilt for the resentment and anger she'd felt for him all those years ago. He *couldn't* be dead.

"See?" Danny pointed at a single skid mark that ran parallel to the road, then veered sharply toward the right. "And like I said, there isn't any a sign of someone down there. The owner probably managed to bail before the bike went over and hitched a ride to town."

Tessa peered over the edge and fought back a sudden wave of nausea, imagining how terrifying it would be to crash like this. Far below, a trail of broken saplings and underbrush led to a crumpled and all-too familiar Harley.

She swallowed hard, trying not to envision Josh, broken and bloody, his engaging laugh silenced forever. "The owner could've been thrown a good distance away."

"Maybe." Danny paced the side of the road. "But

there's no easy way to get down there, and we've got a good view."

"Here." Tessa tied the end of her rope to a tree and tossed the coils out into space. "Hurry!"

Danny quickly descended, while she took out her cell phone and called 911, giving the exact location. Then she slung her rifle over her shoulder and followed him, wishing she'd exchanged her western boots for a pair of good ones meant for hiking.

Brambles and sharp rocks tore at her clothes as she slowly made her way down. Her leather-soled boots slipped and she clung desperately to the rope and an outcropping for a moment to catch her breath.

Once she hit the ground, she hurried over to the motorcycle, where Danny was crouching by the back tire. "The sheriff can check out the license plate," he said. "But what do you think—should we go through these saddle bags? Maybe there's some sort of identification."

His words seemed to be coming from a hundred miles away as she stared at the bike she'd ridden on so many times back in college, her arms wrapped around Josh's flat, muscular midsection and her cheek resting against his broad back.

It was his motorcycle, she had no doubt. The sinking sensation in her stomach nearly overwhelmed her. But dusk was settling fast. In a half hour, just making it back up that steep incline would be nearly impossible, and there was no time for emotion now.

"Let's check those later," she managed. "We need

all the daylight we can get, if we're going to find this guy." She pointed to the north. "Start over there—just go back and forth, slowly, and keep calling out for him. I'll do the same here."

They scoured the area, fanning out wider and wider, until the light faded. Tessa tripped over a hidden stump and pitched forward into a scattering of rocks and downed branches. Something sharp bit into her palm and she cried out.

Danny appeared out of the gloom and hunkered down at her side. "Are you all right?"

"Fine—just a scrape." She pressed two fingers against her palm to stop the bleeding.

"Maybe we should just give up," Danny said. "It's too dark to see, and like I said, I really don't think anybody's down here. When the sheriff comes, maybe he can call for a search and rescue dog."

Logic told her that Danny was right, yet she just couldn't walk away. Not yet. "I think that motorcycle belongs to an old friend, and I need to look a little longer. I just wish I'd thought to bring a flashlight, but I didn't think we'd be down here this long."

"I'll go up and get one." He glanced up towards the highway. "Where's that deputy, anyway?"

"Busy, I'm sure." Again, she began her painstaking search, half afraid she might trip over a body in the dark. Trying hard to fight back her memories of the crushing grief she'd felt years ago.

She'd never wanted to see Josh Bryant again.

Yet right now, she'd give anything to see him alive and well.

Five minutes passed.

Ten.

Fifteen.

The moon was just a sliver and cast faint light that filtered weakly through the heavy pine branches above.

A bright beam of a light bounced crazily through the trees and soon Danny was at her side.

"I could only find one flashlight," he said, his voice somber. "But honestly—I think this is a waste of time."

The hair at the back of her neck prickled. "Did you hear that?"

They both froze. After a long pause, Danny shook his head. "Maybe it's just a marmot."

"At this elevation? I don't think we're high enough." She heard another distant branch snap. "And that would have to be a world-class sized rodent."

"Maybe a coyote, then." He started walking. "If it's a bear, we'd better get *outta* here. Did you hear the news last week? A bear strolled into a campsite and mauled a twelve-year-old girl—dragged her right out of her sleeping bag, and that wasn't more than five miles from here. Three adults had trouble scaring it off, and the DNR still hasn't tracked down that bear."

"Wait."

She heard the sound again. The rustle of underbrush. Another twig snapping. She tensed. "Hello? Is anyone out there?"

Danny paled, no doubt reliving the attack he'd experienced a few years back, but he stood his ground.

"Here you go, Danny." She unsnapped the can of bear repellent from her belt and tossed it to him, then cradled her rifle across her chest and turned on her flashlight. "Go up to the truck and watch for the deputy's patrol car."

He glanced around, then stared in the direction from where they'd heard the noise. "You oughta come, too."

"I can't leave until I finish checking this out, and I need to do it now."

"But—"

"Go, Danny. I had to park quite a way down the road, so it could take that deputy a while to figure out where we are. The faster we get some help, the better."

She watched him disappear into the gloom, then listened for sound of his ascent up the cliff face. When he yelled out that he'd made it to the top, she breathed a sigh of relief.

Turned.

And heard the sound of something thrashing through the brush...coming closer.

FOUR

Tessa stilled and slowly moved her rifle from the crook of her arm into a ready position. Easing sideways, she toed at the dried grass underfoot to avoid stepping on anything that would make noise.

A sudden, fitful breeze eddied through the trees, bringing with it the unmistakable coppery scent of blood. Her stomach lurched when the breeze picked up and the scent grew stronger, more cloying. *Josh?*

She wavered.

Not wanting to go farther.

Knowing she had to, if there was still a chance that he could still be alive. *Please Lord, if this is Josh, let him be all right. Help me bring him out of this safely.*

After a brief silence, she again heard the sound of something crashing through the brush, heading her way.

Biting her lip, she moved more quickly, whispering a constant litany of prayer. If she could smell blood, any cougar, bear or coyote in the vicinity could, too—and it was a blatant an invitation to a free meal.

Now, as she stepped around a rocky ledge, the odor hit her full-force, triggering a gagging reflex and making her stomach roil. And then, barely visible in the dim light, she saw it—a bloodied, mangled… corpse?

She bit back a cry. Swung the flashlight into position and swept it across…

A large buck.

Likely, road kill that had gone over the edge of the highway, then dragged itself into the brush, given the odd angle of its hind legs. And if her guess was right, something big already had dibs on the carcass, and would fight to the death to defend its meal.

She moved back, intending to give the deer wide berth and rapidly put it between her and the oncoming predator.

Her boot hit something more yielding than the rocky, hard-packed ground. She angled the flashlight down…and this time, couldn't hold back a scream.

A pale, outstretched arm was lying in her path.

"Josh—can you hear me? Josh!"

A wave of pain rolled through him when someone grabbed at his shoulder and shook it. Insistent. Demanding. He fought his way up through a suffocating blanket of confusion and pain, then let himself slip back into the deep comfort of oblivion.

"No," that same voice whispered. "You've got to wake up. *Now!"*

The voice was oddly familiar, though her words

seemed to ricochet inside his head without any real meaning. He groaned. Then forced his eyes open and found himself looking up into a face lit with eerie highlights and shadows by a flashlight laying on the ground.

All around was darkness.

"Look, I know you're hurt. You've lost a lot of blood. But you've got to get up. *Now.* We're in a very bad place here. I have no doubt that a bear picked up our scents a long time ago, and that it's very close by. Understand?"

Tessa? He nodded—just once. The motion set off a renewed explosion of fireworks in his skull.

"Help is coming. We just need to get as far away from that bear's meal as we can."

Confusion swirled through his thoughts as she somehow dragged him to his feet and thrust a long, straight branch into his hand. She draped his other arm over her shoulders. One step. Another. Each sent a shock wave of pain through his damaged leg, despite the makeshift splint he'd made earlier.

The bear was at the road kill now—he could hear the sounds of ripping flesh—and then it fell silent.

Sniffing the air, maybe, and rising on his hind legs.

The bear grunted as it crashed forward through the brush, then halted—a false charge, probably, intended to warn away any competition.

Though an empty threat didn't guarantee the next charge wouldn't be for real.

"Can you stand on your own?" Tessa said sharply.

She loomed closer for a quick look at his face, then propped him against a tree. "Stay put."

A faint wash of moonlight filtered through the overheard canopy. He could see her pull her rifle from her shoulder and double check its load.

The bear was close enough that Josh could detect its strong odor now, and he could hear it coming straight at them.

"Hang on," Tessa said. "I don't think either of us is ready to wrestle any bears in the dark."

She aimed at the sky and the crack of rifle fire cut through the darkness like an explosion.

Silence.

Then she fired again and the bear beat a hasty retreat, barreling through the trees like a runaway bulldozer.

"That bought us time, but we still need to get out of here."

"You're…right," he managed, trying to focus on where she stood.

But the ghostly pale birch trees started to shimmer and sway, and the stars spun in the sky as the sharp report of the rifle magnified. Filled the terrain with mortar explosions and billowing sand and a deadly rain of rock and engine parts and bodies…and screams.

Always the terrified, agonizing screams.

His vision dimmed. And when he hit the ground, the earth felt like a welcoming embrace.

Tessa sat on a hard plastic chair in the emergency room waiting area, offering a sympathetic smile to a young mother trying to calm the screaming baby in her arms.

Standing up, she paced the small room, then went to the emergency room doors and stepped outside to breathe the cool night air.

"Ms. McAllister? Is that you?" A young nurse hurried to Tessa's side. "You aren't leaving, are you?"

Tessa turned, her melancholy thoughts turning to fear in an instant. "Is something wrong?"

"They're taking your friend into surgery. The surgeon wants to talk to you, right now."

"Me?"

Nodding, the nurse spun on her heel and hurried away through the double doors marked No Admittance, and led Tessa to the first triage room, where Josh lay on a gurney with IV tubes dangling above him and a digital monitor marking his heart rhythm.

Dark bruises were already forming on the right side of his face. A laceration angling from his forehead to temple had been closed with butterfly bandages—the wounds a garish contrast to his pale, almost gray skin.

His eyes were closed. He lay perfectly still.

And it took very little imagination to imagine that he was already dead.

She'd once felt nothing but anger toward him, but now all she wanted was to see his long, dark lashes flutter open and to see those hazel eyes sparkle with laughter. *Please God, be with him. Help him make it through this.*

A middle-aged woman in a white lab coat, with a stethoscope dangling around her neck, stepped away from the bed and offered her hand. "I'm Dr. West. Mr. Bryant said that he has no relatives here. I understand you're a friend."

A friend. She was hardly that, but she understood the situation. "I guess so."

Two orderlies appeared at the door. At the doctor's nod, they bustled into the room and began preparing the gurney for transport. Within seconds, they'd wheeled him away.

"Josh has signed a release allowing us to share his information with you. The CT scan shows significant damage to his spleen. We can sometimes achieve healing through bed rest, but this looks like a Grade III injury. Given his lab values and escalating heart rate, this bleed is just too big for that."

The woman's words seemed to be coming from far, far away. Tessa blinked and tried to focus. "So you'll have to take it out? Isn't that bad?"

"A total splenectomy would place him at much higher risk for infections, so we'll first go for a more conservative approach and try to repair it. Our orthopedist needs to surgically repair the tibia and fibula fractures. Your friend is actually a very lucky guy, from what I hear about that accident scene."

She tipped her head toward the X-rays mounted on a lighted screen, and even from a distance, Tessa could see multiple fractures just above Josh's ankle.

"Just sit tight," Dr. West continued. "He has a good

chance of coming through all of this without any permanent repercussions. Do you have any questions?"

"Just a good chance?" Tessa asked, feeling faint. "Only that?"

"There's always risk with sustained blood loss. He's shocky, so it's urgent that we get that internal bleeding stopped, STAT." The surgeon glanced at the clock on the wall. "They're getting him prepped, and I need to get up there. The nurses will keep you informed."

"Th-thanks."

"By the way, the secretary has tried calling his family members out East, but she hasn't had any luck so far. You'll be here after surgery is over?"

Tessa nodded.

"It'll probably take a couple hours, depending on what we find, and then he'll be in recovery for at least an hour." Dr. West gave her a sympathetic smile. "If you want to run home and change your clothes or get something to eat, you'll have time. The nurses can loan you some scrubs."

Clothes? Tessa looked back at her, feeling a flash of confusion.

"From what I hear, you saved his life, you know. You can be very proud of that." She rested a gentle hand on Tessa's shoulder. "I know this has been a stressful night."

After the doctor hurried out of the room, Tessa glanced at herself in the mirror over the sink in the corner and drew in a sharp breath.

Under the harsh lighting, her blood-stained shirt

and jeans were an all-too vivid reminder of her frantic efforts to stem the flow of blood from Josh's leg.

The emergency vehicles had arrived twenty minutes after she'd found him semiconscious, his jeans and shirt soaked in blood, and his makeshift bandages doing little to stop the bleeding.

Somehow, she'd completely blanked out on her own appearance until now.

Feeling as if she were moving through a dream where the earth had just tilted sideways, she shivered and reached for the back of a chair, her hands clammy.

It had been a long time since she'd regularly talked to God. Given her faltering faith and anger at Him, maybe He didn't even want to hear from her now.

He probably wouldn't bother to help, because He sure hadn't years ago when she'd needed him most.

But seeing those orderlies wheel Josh away filled her with the most overwhelming fear she'd ever felt in her life since…

Shoving those memories away, she gripped the back of the chair tighter and choked back the tears clogging her throat.

Dear God—please, please help him. Not for my sake, but for his. Please…

Josh shifted his weight awkwardly, hampered by the heavy cast on his left leg and IV line taped to his arm. The last two days had passed in a medication-induced blur of drowsiness, interspersed with visits by nurses who prodded and poked and took his temperature every hour, and lab techs who seemed to take special pleasure in drawing endless vials of blood.

This morning, he'd agreed to nothing stronger than Tylenol, wanting to keep his mind clear. Now, with Sheriff Michael Robinson standing at the side of his bed, he was thankful for that decision.

The tall, dark-haired man reached out and shook Josh's hand. "I've stopped in a couple times," he said. "But you were always asleep or off having some sort of test. How are you feeling today?"

"Like I was run over by a bulldozer. But better than yesterday, anyhow. The doc says she'll release me tomorrow."

A groove deepened in the man's cheek, and Josh's fingers subconsciously flexed, needing to grasp a camera that could capture those craggy, rugged facial lines.

Alarm rushed through him and he struggled to sit up, then fell back, weak and exhausted. "My... cameras..."

"My deputy has all of your things in lock-up at the station. All safe—unless the crash impact damaged anything." The sheriff glanced down at the clipboard in his hand, then he gave Josh an easy smile that didn't mask the intensity in his gaze. "What brought you out here?"

"Photo assignment."

"Newspaper?"

"*Green Earth*—a magazine. My...ID card is in my billfold."

The sheriff looked down at his papers and frowned. "We didn't find one at the scene. The ER nurses say it wasn't with the clothes you were wearing, either."

Josh closed his eyes, thinking about the four credit cards he carried, plus other personal information… and his last photo of his fiancée, Lara, taken just hours before a roadside bombing took her life.

"It would've been in my back right pocket."

"I'll send a deputy out to the scene and have him look. Soooo…how long have you been in the area?"

The man's tone was a little too folksy, and Josh suddenly knew that there was more than just an accident report on that clipboard. "I get the feeling you've done a background check on me already," he said quietly. "Find anything interesting, Sheriff?"

A brief smile flickered at the corner of Michael's mouth. "Nothing on record…though not everything is, usually."

"Can I ask why you'd need to do that? Or is it protocol on anyone who ends up in this hospital?"

"How long have you been in Wyoming?" Michael's voice hardened. "And where were you staying?"

Uneasy now, Josh shifted against the pillows. "I've been in the Wolf Creek area for a little over a week. I have—or did have—a campsite, west of the Snow Canyon Ranch property line."

Michael pinned him with an intense look. "How would you know where that is, exactly?"

Some of his memories from just before the accident were still hazy, and now Josh frowned. "I—I'm not sure."

"You know the McAllisters?"

"Tessa, from college. I—I knew she used to live around here, but we never kept in touch." At the sheriff's satisfied expression, Josh realized the man must've already talked to Tessa, and was just checking for inconsistencies in Josh's story. "You can check my credit card charges, if you want. There'll be gas station charges starting in Washington, D.C., a week ago. You can also call Sylvia Meiers at the magazine. Her number is…" he searched his memory, and came up blank. "It's probably in my…"

"Billfold?"

"I'm afraid so."

Michael cleared his throat. "Can you remember anything about your accident?"

"Not everything. I remember coming up on a sharp curve in the road, and suddenly found a moose crossing the road. I don't remember if I actually hit it, or if I just swerved and left the road."

"You're sure it was an animal?" Michael frowned. "Not another vehicle?"

"When you look death in the face, time seems to stand still." Josh closed his eyes, thinking back. Envisioned the moment when he'd taken that corner. "I don't have any doubt. Why?"

Michael jotted a few notes on the clipboard, then looked up. "We've had some problems around here lately, and that same afternoon there was a break-in at a cabin not far from there. It wouldn't be a surprise if the suspects were in a big hurry to leave."

Josh settled back against the pillow, suddenly tired. And unsettled, because if a simple conversation wore him out, what on earth was he going to do when the hospital discharged him?

"What you've said confirms what I heard from the Bassetts…a couple of guys who happened to be fishing in the area. They mentioned seeing a moose near the highway in that vicinity, too." Michael studied him intently for a few moments. "You're a very lucky man," he said finally. "I hear you wouldn't have made it if Tessa hadn't found you when she did."

"It was a toss-up, I guess. Internal bleeding or a bear."

"And I understand you don't have relatives here. Have you made arrangements to go home?"

Home. A mostly empty condominium on the outskirts of Washington, D.C. A place he landed rarely, between photo assignments abroad. Two flights of stairs. No elevator.

He didn't even want to think about the indignity of trying to manage those steps with a cast and crutches, much less trying to make the trip up and down with groceries and other supplies.

"I'm not sure where I'll go, or how I'll get there. I understand my Harley is totaled."

"We hauled it up to a dealer over in Jackson. He says it can be fixed, if you're interested." Michael pulled a business card out of his uniform shirt pocket.

"I'm not sure what your insurance deductible is, but he says the repairs are possible, and I know that people around here are generally happy with his work." He smiled. "Then again, maybe you'd rather fly or rent a car to make your trip home a little easier."

Josh shook his head. "I've had that bike since college. It belonged to my late uncle, and I'd do just about anything to rebuild it. I'll stick around these parts until it's ready to roll."

"You probably won't find any lodging. The resorts around here fill up months in advance."

The sheriff was right. Josh had been checking into rental property in the area—the seasonal lodges and cabins, as well as the long-term lease situations. Not only was everything exorbitantly priced, but it had all been spoken for months ago—even Snow Canyon Lodge and Cabins, which he'd learned was operated by the sheriff and his new wife.

"I'd be careful, if I were you." Michael paused, as if debating about how much to say. "Did Tessa tell you that someone shot at her a couple weeks ago?"

"What?"

"She was on a trail close to one of the break-ins. Someone in a dark pickup shot her in the leg, but she managed to make it home all right. I brought in the state police to help process the crime scene at the cabin."

Josh had felt uneasy before, but now a sick feeling worked through his stomach. "Someone *shot* at her? Do you have any suspects?"

"Not yet. We're not sure if it was accidental, a warning shot gone wrong, or someone taking intentional aim. I just wish I knew if it was one of the cabin thieves who have been hitting the area. If the guy recognized her and thought she saw something incriminating, he could decide to go after her again."

"But she has ranch hands at her place for protection, right? Other employees?"

"Just one old man, and a young guide who goes out there whenever he has a pack trip." Michael sighed. "I think she needs to stay with someone until this is settled, but my wife and I offered, and she refused. She's just too stubborn for her own good."

A career as a photojournalist had drawn Josh to hot spots around the globe; and more dangerous situations than most people ever encountered. But the thought of Tessa at a remote ranch, alone and defenseless against some unseen enemy, filled him with more fear than he'd felt in a long, long time.

He knew she wasn't happy about him turning up in her life again—she'd made that crystal clear. But *someone* needed to be out there, protecting her.

Michael pocketed his pen and dropped his clipboard to his side. "I'd better leave. You look stressed out—like you could use a nap."

"And that's just so sad, isn't it? I haven't taken naps since I was three," Josh retorted dryly. "Believe me, I can't wait to get back on my feet."

But when he did, he wouldn't be setting up camp out in the woods. He needed to figure out a way to wrangle an invitation to Snow Canyon Ranch, because Tessa needed help, and an injured guy on crutches was better than no one at all.

FIVE

Tessa took a deep breath, unclenched her fists, then walked into the hospital with a determined smile fixed on her face.

This was the last place she wanted to be. It had taken her ten minutes of slow, concentrated breathing to walk in the door of the building. But after Michael's phone call this morning, she knew it was the right thing to do—even if it made her heart pound and her palms sweat. *I can do this. I can handle Josh for a few weeks.*

She knocked on Josh's door and stepped just inside, one hand on the door frame. He rolled his head on the pillow and looked at her, his eyes widening in surprise. The bruises and cuts on his face still made him look as if he'd been in a fight and lost, and her heart softened...just a little.

"I understand you'll be released tomorrow," she said. "Though Michael says you plan to stay in town until your Harley is fixed so you can ride it home."

"True." A hint of amusement glimmered in Josh's

eyes, undoubtedly at her obvious discomfort. "And now that a deputy found my billfold, I can actually pay for it."

"It's probably almost impossible to find lodging around here, this time of year."

"After making endless phone calls, I know that's true." His expression grew forlorn. "I guess I'll have to stay in my tent—if it's still where I left it."

"Sounds like a perfect place, what with those surgical sutures and a cast to keep clean." She drew in a steadying breath. "The nurses tell me that you're using a wheelchair for now, but that you'll graduate to crutches before discharge."

"Lucky me," he said with a dry laugh.

"I talked to my housekeeper Sofia, and we figure the bunkhouse at the ranch would work, if we could get you up the porch steps. We made it into a rustic sort of cabin duplex years ago, and she and Gus live in the bigger unit at the east end—but the other side is empty."

"Really?"

She tried for a believable smile. "We can even bring you your meals."

"You're sure you won't mind having me around?"

"Look, we were…friends, once. We broke up. End of story. But since I'm probably the only person you know around here, I can certainly help you out."

He hesitated. "It's kind of you, but…"

"What other options do you have? You need a place to stay, and I have the room. Claire—my mother—

stays with my sister Janna and her husband Michael, and I'm not around the home place all that much. But Sofia will be close by, so she can watch over you, and help with anything you need if I'm not there."

He studied her face for a long moment, as if reading her thoughts. "Thanks," he said finally. "I understand I also need to thank you for saving my life. I don't remember much about that night, but if you hadn't come looking for me—if you hadn't persisted—I wouldn't be here today."

"Thank Danny for noticing the skid marks on the highway, and the doctor who came in for your emergency surgery, not me." She knew she sounded ungracious, but this was the most awkward situation she'd faced in a long time. "I'll be here tomorrow at noon to pick you up."

"I'll repay you," he said quietly. "I promise you that."

"No need, just heal well and get better." She managed a smile and excused herself, then left the hospital as quickly as possible.

It was the right thing to do. Her sister Leigh, a veterinarian in town, lived in a small apartment at the back of her vet clinic and had no space for a guest. Janna and Michael's resort was fully booked—and even if they had room, Claire lived there. If she even caught wind of the fact that Josh was in town, there was no telling what she would do, but it certainly wouldn't be pretty.

On the long drive back to the ranch, Tessa found

herself talking to God again. A gentle warmth seemed to spread through her as she spoke from her heart.

Please—let this all work out without anyone being hurt. And please, help me keep my secrets safe.

"Quite a place," Josh said, tilting a glance at Tessa as she drove up the mile-long lane leading to the home place of Snow Canyon Ranch.

After leaving the highway, the road dropped into a broad valley sectioned into pastures of horses and ghost-white Charlois cattle, then wound back up into the foothills, through heavy stands of pine and aspen. Now, the roofs of the house and barns were just visible over the next rise.

The rugged, snow-frosted peaks of the Rockies formed a stunning backdrop as far to the north and south as the eye could see.

She shrugged. "It's a working ranch. Nothing fancy like those horse farms out East. But I don't think there's any place else as pretty as this." She spared him a quick look. "Are you doing okay?"

"Great." He used both hands to readjust the position of his left leg, though in the confines of the truck cab he was able to gain just a few inches at best.

At the hospital he'd been in bed or in a wheelchair, with his cast elevated, and after twenty-five miles of rough, twisting mountain road—much of it potholed or cobbled together with patches of asphalt—his throbbing leg felt painfully tight inside the cast.

If he'd had his hunting knife on his belt, he might've

been tempted to start carving away the hard fiberglass, just to gain some relief.

After negotiating a tight turn, Tessa glanced at him again. The corner of her mouth lifted briefly before settling back into a grim line. "I can well imagine how great you feel. If I had a car, I would've driven it instead. Might've been smoother."

"I'm just thankful for a place to stay." *And for more reasons than you know.*

He'd been careful to avoid sounding too relieved over her offer of a place to recuperate. In truth, it had been an answer to his prayers. He'd been mulling over a dozen different ways to finagle a way to stay at her ranch, and none of them had seemed plausible enough to broach.

"I know this isn't exactly convenient for you," he added.

"Like I said at the hospital, it's no problem. Ray, my other ranch hand, quit last week, so his side of the bunkhouse is empty."

"You aren't hiring someone else?"

She snorted under her breath. "Take a look. A good look. What do you see?"

He surveyed the panorama of ranch land unfolding as they topped the last rise. "Cattle. Horses. Trees—lots of trees. A big ranch house and set of outbuildings. Nice place, by the way."

She gestured impatiently. "Look *closer.*"

Despite the deep green blanket of trees cloaking the lower half of the mountains, the grass at either side of the ranch land was pale gold, and looked dry enough to shatter in a stiff breeze. He caught a faint, acrid scent of smoke coming in through the truck windows—probably from the forest fires that had been escalating to the north and west.

The effect of the drought was worse here than any place he'd seen yet.

"I suppose all of the ranchers around here are hurting."

"For five years and counting." She nodded toward the cattle. "Last summer we got just one cutting of hay instead of three, and I had to buy several loads out of Nebraska. If it weren't for our government grazing rights on the higher ranges, we'd have had to ship our entire herd by now. As much as I need another cowhand, not paying those extra wages for a few weeks has been a blessing."

He studied the tall, rangy cattle closest to the fence. They didn't bother looking back at the truck. "Doesn't look like they have much grass."

"I need to move them up into their summer range as soon as possible, assuming I can find someone to help."

"You run this entire ranch with *one* employee?"

Again, that faint flicker of a smile that made him wish he could bring back the beautiful smile he remembered from their college days. "Yep."

She drove across the wide, graveled parking area between the barns and the fenced yard surrounding the main house, and pulled to a stop next to a log building set back in a stand of pines. It was a good fifty feet long, with porches at both ends and cheerful red curtains at all eight of the multipaned windows facing the road. "Cabin One" and "Cabin Two" had been carved into small wooden signs hung at either end of the building.

"You've met Danny—he's our seasonal guide. He only takes pack trips as scheduled, so he doesn't live here. Otherwise, it's just Gus, Sofia and me."

A grizzled old man hobbled out onto the porch of Cabin Two, at the east end of the bunkhouse, shielding his eyes against the cool, late May sunshine. His faded jeans looked as old as he did; his bright purple Colorado Rockies T-shirt an incongruent contrast to his battered western straw hat and dusty boots.

"That's *him?*"

Tessa nodded as she opened her door and stepped out of the truck. "Gus worked for my mother before I was born."

Levering himself out of the truck cab, Josh collected his crutches and shoved the door shut. He held his breath as Gus tentatively navigated the stairs of the porch one halting step at a time. "How old *is* he?"

"He won't tell." She watched Gus with obvious affection. "Now and then Sofia and I try to convince him to retire, but he won't do that either, so he mostly helps here at the home place. He usually moves better than that, but his horse fell on him yesterday."

Josh winced, imagining those lean, brittle old

bones crushed beneath twelve-hundred pounds of horseflesh.

"Before you say it—no, I didn't think he should be putting in a day on horseback. But Gus has a mind of his own, and he won't give an inch when it comes to avoiding something because of his age."

When Gus finally reached Tessa's truck, the razor sharp glitter in his narrowed eyes certainly didn't reflect any desire for sympathy. "So, you brought him here, after all."

"Just as we discussed," she said evenly. "He won't be in the way. We'll just set an extra plate."

Gus snorted, holding Josh's gaze with a fierce, protective expression for a long moment—a clear masculine challenge—before turning to grab Josh's duffel bag out of the back of the truck.

He limped his way up the steps at the west end of the building. "Changed the sheets. Brought towels. Ain't a resort, but it oughta do."

Josh awkwardly ascended the steps with his crutches, hopping on one foot, all too aware that Tessa was right behind him in case he fell.

That alone forced him on, even after his cast rapped sharply against the edge of the top step, sending waves of pain ricocheting up his leg.

From the open doorway, Gus watched his approach with his arms clamped over his chest, and Josh had the distinct feeling that Gus would enjoy seeing him end up in a heap in the dirt—and would be even happier if Josh simply packed up and left.

Odd behavior, for a man he'd never met until today. But then, he hadn't exactly felt friendly vibes
from Tessa, either.

"You know," he said as he finally made it up to the
porch. "This probably wasn't such a good idea.
Maybe I should just—"

The porch started to tilt. Dark spots swam in front
of his eyes...

And then the bright sunshine turned to black.

Please, God, help me get through this.

Tessa's silent prayer probably didn't surprise God,
but it certainly surprised her. After a decade of stony
silence on her part, she needed help—and needed it
from a Higher Source. Fast.

And it was all because of the man stretched out
on the rustic, pine-framed sofa in Cabin One, who
was now regarding her with troubled eyes.

"I *never* pass out," he muttered, his voice hoarse.

"Of course not."

"I—" Confusion flashed in his eyes. "I..."

"You fainted dead away on the stairs a few minutes ago. Gus and I hauled you in here, and we're
both hoping you'll agree to stay horizontal."

He reached up to touch the back of his head and
his frown deepened. "But..."

"I caught you, but—hey, what are you now, six-
two, two hundred plus? We went down like a felled
tree. It could've been much worse, but you'll probably
have a bump on the back of your head tomorrow."

So would she, along with bruises on her back and shoulder after trying to cushion his fall, but he didn't need to know that.

"Sorry." He shook his head sharply as if to clear his thoughts, then winced.

"I called the ER a minute ago. They said they told you to avoid stairs for the next ten days and to be really quiet, given the type of surgery you had. Also, they told me that they gave you some prescription pain meds before you left, and those can make you foggy." She leaned forward in her chair and tapped the patient instruction sheets laying on the pine coffee table. "I found these on the floor of my truck. You should've told me before we tried getting you in here."

"I think those meds must've hit on the way out here. I…" He frowned. "I usually don't take anything stronger than Tylenol."

A corner of his mouth lifted in a woozy smile, and with that boyish lock of dark hair tipping over his forehead and those dark, thick eyelashes, she could imagine him as a child. One who'd probably been able to charm himself out of trouble every time.

Maybe that charm had worked on her back in college, but it would have no impact on her now. *None.* She was going to get through these next weeks just fine, and then happily wave goodbye.

She leaned back in her chair. "Gus went to feed the livestock. Now that you aren't looking quite as groggy, I need to go help him. You'll be okay?"

He nodded.

"You'll stay put? On this sofa until I get back?"

His weak smile widened. "You betcha."

A laugh escaped before she could catch it. "You betcha? Where've you been all these years, Minnesota?"

"Middle East, mos'ly," he mumbled. The flash of humor in his eyes faded. "My Lara was from Minnesota. Fiancée…til she died."

Fiancée? And the poor woman had *died?*

Tessa had been angry at him for years over his blissful ignorance of what had happened to her, but apparently he'd encountered sorrow, too.

She backed away, feeling an odd flutter in her stomach at the thought of his fiancée. Of course he would've had girlfriends all these years. Maybe even a couple of marriages and divorces, after his fiancée passed away.

Perhaps his significant other or some family members were in the midst of catching flights to Wyoming, ready to bundle him up and take him home.

It's not my business. Don't meddle where you were never wanted.

She hesitated, then turned on her heel, resolutely left the cabin and headed for the barn.

She'd quit loving him long ago. It didn't matter at all what he did—or with whom. She'd made a good life for herself and had no desire to muddy up her future with any more romantic relationships.

After several that had gone nowhere, she'd learned that they just weren't worth the time.

SIX

Yesterday, Tessa had spent most of the day on horseback searching for her missing cattle. Again, to no avail.

Now, she was sitting across a desk from a loan officer at the Wolf Creek Bank—someone who held the future of Snow Canyon Ranch in a single manila folder—and wished she could be anywhere else.

The woman's name—Ellen Miller—wasn't familiar. Which, all things considered, might be a good thing. Someone new to the area couldn't have had any run-ins with Claire over the years.

The woman drummed her fingertips on the folder. "An extension?"

Claire's all-too familiar words from the past filtered into Tessa's thoughts. *Act like you already won hands down—and only a fool will stand in your way.*

Tessa lifted her chin. "That's right."

"On a twelve-thousand dollar loan for…" Ellen flipped the folder open and withdrew a computer printout. "Cattle?"

"Breeding stock. An infusion of a new genetic line we—"

The woman waved a hand sharply in dismissal. "I understand you've lost cattle to theft recently."

Surprised, Tessa settled back in her chair. "We found thirty head, but ten are still missing. Why?"

"Are any of these *missing* cattle from this line?"

"Three."

Ellen fixed a narrowed gaze on Tessa's face. "And what, exactly, have you done about it?"

Tessa fought back a wave of irritation at the woman's supercilious tone. "The loss wasn't carelessness. Someone cut a remote fence line. I reported the loss to the sheriff immediately. Then I faxed detailed descriptions of each missing animal's color, markings, ear notches and registered brand to sales barns in four states. None of them have been auctioned so far."

"So you simply *lost* them."

"They could still be on national forest land or blended into someone else's herd. Or they could be in someone's freezer."

"And you don't have insurance on your herd?"

"You and I both know how expensive it would be for a thousand cattle and a horse herd. It just isn't feasible, except on our bulls and senior stallion."

The faintest of smiles touched the woman's thin mouth. "Sound business principles would say otherwise, dear."

Dear? Tessa narrowed her eyes. This loan officer

was probably in her early forties, and her condescension was the last straw. "I think you'd discover that few ranchers in this county agree with you. In an ideal world, maybe, but not in everyday practice. Now, about that loan?"

The woman made a tsk-tsk sound as she closed the manila folder. "I'm afraid there's really nothing I can do, because that contract was your legal agreement to pay on time. I did try—but our bank manager said no. He referred to another loan you had...a year ago?"

Tessa blinked. "We were three weeks late. My mother was hospitalized, and until that time she still insisted on handling all of the business at the ranch. I wasn't even aware of that due date until the reminder notice came."

"I'm sorry." She stood up in obvious dismissal. "The current note is due the twenty-sixth of June. Is there anything else?"

Tessa had expected as much, but the situation still rankled. If not for the drought, cattle prices over the past year, and the tractor she'd had to replace, there wouldn't have been a problem. "You'll get your money on time."

Her fists clenched at her sides, Tessa pasted a cool smile on her face, spun on her heel, and walked out into the lobby of the bank. She was halfway to the entrance when she heard someone call her name.

"Well, if it isn't Tessa McAllister." Arlen Foreman sauntered toward her from his place in line at one of the teller windows. He was tall, elegant, and easily pushing sixty, with neatly trimmed white hair and mustache, and as usual, he was wearing his ever-present Indiana Jones fedora.

She'd always suspected that he wore it for rakish effect—just another bit of showboating for the customers who used his upscale wilderness outfitting company. "Arlen."

"So," he said, the sharp, assessing glint in his eyes at odds with his overly friendly smile. "I suppose you're ready for a big season this year?"

"I hope it's a good one. High gas prices really hurt us last year."

"Really." He chuckled. "I suppose you have a lot of those lower-end clients out at your place."

Tessa bristled at the insult. Yet he was probably right, in a way—he offered the luxury condos, a swimming pool, and a chef at the upscale ranch that served as a base camp for his company.

She had a housekeeper who doubled as a cook when needed and no extra lodging facilities—other than her sister's resort, which was a good forty-five minutes away—and Snow Canyon Ranch Outfitters was hardly likely to attract the crowd that arrived in private Lear jets.

He leaned in close and winked. "Don't forget my offer, sweetheart. It's still stands."

"It won't happen, Arlen." At the corner of her eye, she saw Ellen Miller standing at the door of her private office, her arms folded across her chest. "At least, not any time soon."

The walls of the lobby seemed to close in on her, making it difficult to breathe. "Nice seeing you."

Without waiting for his reply, Tessa strode out of the bank to her pickup, climbed inside and rested her forehead against the steering wheel.

Arlen she could handle, despite his pompous attitude and determination to buy her out. She'd find a way to come up with the loan money on time, to prove Ellen wrong.

But Arlen hadn't been far off-base about her fledgling business. This would be her third season, and she was still operating on a shoestring. How many customers did she lose each year to the glamorous websites and glossy brochures of her competitors, with their upscale facilities and big advertising budgets? If the economy took a downturn, her numbers would drop even further.

And then, her dreams of financial independence would die.

Josh levered himself off the couch and swung his heavy cast around so he could sit at the edge. Tessa had ordered him to stay put, but she'd based that on the fact that he'd been overmedicated and confused.

He was *much* better now. He was too restless to sit still.

And he couldn't have come up with a better set-up if he'd tried.

He needed a place to recuperate, of course. He'd been concerned for Tessa's safety. But he'd also hoped for just this sort of connection, where he could

insert himself into the fabric of rural Wyoming life
and finish the magazine assignment he'd been given.

It was a perfect, fair arrangement, even if Tessa
didn't know *all* of his reasons for being here.

He glanced around the snug little cabin, with its
pine paneled walls, rustic furniture, and cheerful,
bandana-print curtains. There was a kitchenette of
sorts in one corner; a short counter topped with cup-
boards, flanked with a small refrigerator and a stove
at either end.

Ignoring the crutches propped against the end of
the sofa, he hopped over to the refrigerator and
peered inside, breathing as hard as if he'd just completed a five-mile run. The motion kicked up the pain
deep in his belly. Bracing one hand on the counter,
he doubled over his other forearm, realizing that
maybe—just this one time—Tessa might have been
right about him staying on the sofa. After three days
here, he still wasn't up to doing much.

The screen door to the porch squealed open and
slammed shut. He turned and found a tall woman
standing just inside, with a cloth-covered tray.

Slender, with an ageless sort of beauty that placed
her somewhere between thirty and fifty, she had an
arresting, regal presence, and once again, he felt the
urge to find his camera and start taking pictures.

Her stern, unyielding expression, lit by late afternoon sunlight filtering through the windows,
would make a perfect study in black and white, but
he had a feeling that she'd never agree to it. In fact,

the surprising amount of antipathy in her dark eyes took him aback.

"Tessa's running errands, so I brought you an early supper," she said. "Since you're up, I'll put it on the table. Eat while it's hot." She set the tray down, leaving it covered, and turned to go.

"Wait."

She turned back slowly, telegraphing her veiled disapproval, and met his gaze squarely. "Yes?"

He tried his most disarming smile. "Thanks. It smells wonderful."

"Is that all?" She stood as still and unyielding as marble, her hands held stiffly at her sides, but she radiated the attitude of someone who wanted to give him a lecture he wouldn't forget.

Maybe, he mused, she had anger management issues and needed therapy. "I'm concerned about Tessa," he said.

Silence.

"I understand there's been trouble out here." At her impassive expression, he added, "The sheriff told me that someone shot at Tess three weeks ago, yet there've been no arrests."

"So why does that concern you?" Sofia's voice was like the crack of a whip, sharp and challenging.

"She was a friend long ago, and she saved my life this week. It sounds like she could be in danger, and I care about her."

The older woman made a low, derisive sound under her breath.

"Okay, then I feel like I owe her. Is that fair enough?"

"You'd best eat and rest, so you can heal and be on your way. *That's* what you can do for her."

He watched the housekeeper turn on her heel and stalk out the door. "Is it just me, or do you and Gus guard her from everyone who comes this way?"

He'd spoken softly, more to himself than to her, but Sofia stopped at the edge of the porch and sent a look over her shoulder that could've skinned a bear at thirty yards, then silently continued down the steps.

So it is me. He hobbled over to the small kitchen table, settled into one of the two wooden chairs, and lifted the napkin from the tray.

Steam wafted the rich aromas from a heated plated stacked with enchiladas and two burritos, and a smaller plate bearing a trio of sugar-crusted buñuelos.

He whistled under his breath as he looked out the window at Sofia marching toward the house. He'd never met her, yet the woman clearly despised him.

But why?

"This was a big mistake, Tess." Gus tossed a bale of hay off the stack in the main horse barn, then climbed down and hoisted it onto two others arranged crosswise on a wheelbarrow. "Mark my words, you'll be sorry you ever let Josh Bryant set foot on this place."

"We won't see him much. Sofia said she'd take his

meals to him, and I'm sure he'll mostly be resting in bed." She trundled the wheelbarrow down the aisle to the first stall, sliced the baling twine, and sectioned off a quarter of a bale for Claire's favorite old mare, Socks. "Anyway, I didn't have much choice. Where would he go?"

"Back to wherever he came from?" Gus took an equal portion and carried it into the next stall. "Coulda hopped on a plane in Jackson."

"Michael said the surgeon was really concerned about him traveling so soon. And anyway, his motorcycle is being rebuilt, and he doesn't want to leave without it. It has a lot of sentimental value to him."

Gus grumbled under his breath as they continued down the aisle, delivering hay to each stall. "You gonna have your mother over tomorrow, like usual?"

"I...don't know."

"You have any idea what Claire will do if she finds Josh Bryant here?"

Tessa did have a pretty good idea, and it wasn't something she wanted to deal with. On her best days, Claire was demanding, but her slowly advancing dementia had increased that ten-fold.

For years she'd demanded that her three daughters call her Claire. Last week, Tessa had inadvertently called her Mom, and she'd exploded with rage.

"Maybe she won't remember Josh's name."

Gus snorted. "It's recent history that she forgets, darlin'. Not what happened ten, fifteen years ago."

"Just wishful thinking, I guess," Tessa said on a

long sigh. "She never actually met him...but I can't lie to her, if she asks who he is."

"And you can't go asking that boy to lay low, or you'd have to tell *him* why. Or is that something you maybe oughta do?"

"'That boy' is thirty-five years old, Gus. And old history is just that. Why stir it up?" She grabbed another armload of hay, then looked up and found Gus had stopped to watch her, his expression weary. "There's just no point anymore. Is there?"

"You'd have to tell me. Would it be better to finally just get it over?"

"What good would that do?" Tension curled through her stomach, drawing it into a painful knot. "We both know exactly how much Josh cared about me back then. He...he doesn't even deserve to know. And he probably wouldn't care, anyway—which would hurt all the more."

She turned and rested her forehead against the vertical metal bars fronting one of the stalls, closing her eyes as a wave of painful memories flooded back.

She'd gone off to college, freshman year. She fallen helplessly in love with him—the most gorgeous boy she'd ever seen. They'd dated every night, lost in each other, sure it was their once-in-a-lifetime love...

And then one night, they went too far.

They had their first big fight a week later. By the end of spring break, she was facing the terrifying consequences of their careless actions...and Josh had disappeared. Her letters were returned, his phone was disconnected, and he'd essentially dropped from the face of the earth, without ever knowing that he'd left her pregnant.

So she'd had to deal with Claire alone during the next nine months, her shame magnified with every angry glance and disparaging remark. Those months had been the most difficult of her life.

But what followed was even worse…

"You'll do whatever's best, Tessie." Gus came up beside her and rested a gnarled hand on her shoulder. "Sofia and me will always be behind you, a hundred-percent."

He was as close to being a father as anyone ever had been, and she leaned against him for just a moment before stiffening her spine. "Then don't say anything. Maybe it isn't a kindness to tell him, anyway. At least not now."

"Whatever you say." But his voice was troubled as he turned back to finish the chores. He absently rubbed a hand over his heart. "Maybe…you can take Claire for a drive this week instead of coming here?"

But they both knew that she lived for the afternoons when she could come back to her old home at the ranch…and that it was almost impossible to stand in the way of Claire McAllister.

The whole county probably knew how dangerous that could be.

SEVEN

Tessa pulled up to a stop in front of the Snow Canyon Lodge and rested her wrists at the top of the steering wheel, trying to ignore the nervous little tap dance in her stomach.

Her sister Janna stepped out onto the wide, covered porch of the building and waved, so it wasn't possible to just slip away. With a sigh, Tessa climbed out of the truck and started up the long flagstone walk.

It was only fair that all three sisters help with their mother, and Tessa had always done her share. Until last year, Claire had been able to continue living down at the ranch with her. But gradually, dementia had been taking its toll, and now she needed better supervision than Tessa could provide 24/7, given her long hours of ranch work and the overnight pack trips.

Claire had been living at the lodge for almost a year, and she still wasn't happy about her loss of independence.

Janna, her strawberry blond ponytail swinging

with each step, came down to meet Tessa halfway. She looked over her shoulder at the lodge, then bit her lower lip.

"I've been talking all morning about the new calves and foals at the ranch," she said in a low voice. "Maybe you can keep her entertained with checking them all out, then take her to lunch in town."

"I hope so. There's no sense in getting her upset." Tessa sighed. "Though there's no way that I'll be able to keep her away from the home place for the next four weeks, either. And even if she doesn't see Josh, sooner or later, she's going to notice that someone new is living in the old bunkhouse."

"Maybe she'll surprise us. Surely after all these years, even she can find some forgiveness in her heart."

"We're talking about Claire McAllister here. There are people in this town who say she doesn't even have one."

Though even as she spoke those words, Tessa felt a twinge of guilt at her own failings in that department. Josh had been at the ranch for four days now, and she'd tried to avoid him as much as possible.

Janna rested a hand on Tessa's forearm, her eyes sad and filled with concern. "I know it's been hard for you, living at the ranch all these years. She probably ran it—and you—with an iron hand." Janna looked across the lawn to where her ten-year-old daughter Riley was playing fetch with Maggie, her fluffy little white dog. "We've had a taste of that while she's been living with us."

"I'm sure," Tessa said dryly. "After Leigh and Cole get married at the end of June, maybe we can all take turns at having her stay with us for a week or so at a time."

"Actually, I've read that it's better to have a quiet, consistent environment with Alzheimer's patients, so it's probably best for her to stay here…until it's no longer possible."

"I hope that day's long in coming. I think it would kill her if she had to be moved into a nursing home."

"Are…you okay, with Josh being there?"

"It doesn't matter. He means nothing to me anymore. I just stay clear and Sofia takes him his meals."

"But—"

The front door of the lodge opened, and Claire stepped outside. Slender, angular, with the no-nonsense stride and sun-cured skin of a lifelong rancher, she strode toward them. "You're *late*."

Janna met Tessa's eyes, her mouth twitching, as a flash of complete understanding passed between them.

"I had to wait for the farrier," Tessa said briskly. "Ready to go? I figure we'll drive out into some of the pastures to check on the mares and foals, then we can go to the upper range and take a look at the cow-calf herd. I need your advice on which ones we should cull. After that, I need to pick up some horse liniment at Leigh's vet clinic, so I'll take you to lunch at that new café next door. Maybe she can even join us."

With a short nod, Claire continued on toward the

Snow Canyon Ranch pickup and climbed in the passenger side.

Janna gave Tessa a thumbs-up. "You handled that well."

"For once, anyway. Actually, I do need to haul a load of cattle to a sale barn. Soon." Tessa hesitated, still feeling awkward over their closer relationship after years of estrangement. "There's a note due at the bank, and the loan officer refused to even consider an extension."

"For your outfitting business?"

"Breeding stock for the ranch. With everything else that happened this year, money is tight. But if I don't come up with the twelve grand in time, I have a feeling the bank will be happy to collect the collateral and ruin our credit rating."

"One of the perks of being a McAllister in this county—where all too many people still resent us."

"Or Claire. But none of that was our fault. *Ever.*"

It had been Claire, always Claire, and her callous disregard for anyone who stood in her way. She'd always driven a hard bargain. Evicted tenants experiencing tough times. Some said she'd even used her influence with her old cronies at the local bank, to see that several struggling ranchers were foreclosed, so she could snap up their property.

Janna bit her lower lip. "I wish I had the money to give you. But this will be our first full tourist season here, and I invested everything I had into refurbishing this place."

"I wasn't asking, but thanks anyway. I'll figure it out." Tessa pulled her truck keys out of her pocket. "Barring any trouble, I'll have her home by six."

Tessa turned to leave, then sniffed the air and stopped. "Do you smell that?"

Janna glanced to the west, and Tessa followed her gaze.

From here, the faint, silvery-blue plumes of smoke were barely visible—belying the fact that hundreds of acres of tinder-dry forest land were now reduced to cinders.

"There were lightning strikes up in the mountains last night, and also down by Salt Creek," Janna said somberly. "I heard the crews are fighting a half-dozen new fires."

"It's way too early for the fire season to start. What's it going to be like when we get to the beginning of August?"

They looked at each other, and then at the towering pines surrounding the log-framed lodge and the row of rustic guest cabins that trailed over the hill. Every part of the resort was highly vulnerable, and the ranch was, too.

With just one bolt of lightning—or a careless camper's cigarette—everything they'd worked for could go up in smoke.

If he spent another minute indoors, he'd go mad. And if he had to wear this cast much longer, it would probably drive him over the edge, too.

Josh grabbed one of his crutches and hobbled to the door, pulled it open and hopped over to the Adirondack-style chairs on the front porch.

He awkwardly maneuvered into one and propped his foot on the seat of the other, then looked across the broad parking area toward the barns where Danny was talking to a group of middle-aged tourists.

One by one, he helped each person mount a horse and re-checked the girths, then he climbed onto his own rangy buckskin and led them down the road, with a single pack horse in tow indicating that this would be a supper cook-out ride. A cloud of dust boiled up behind them, then they turned off the road and disappeared into the trees.

Tessa had left in her pickup hours before, and Sofia had taken off soon afterward. From the pastures behind the barns came the occasional whinny, and somewhere in the trees above, a woodpecker was jackhammering its way into a tree. But otherwise the solitude was almost deafening—a surreal contrast to Josh's life up until this point.

He had only to close his eyes and he was back.

Back to that arid, dusty and desolate land where roadside bombs threatened the most innocuous trips. Where one could die in a split second if caught in the crosshairs of the sniper's rifle or in the vicinity of someone willing to blow themselves up for their cause.

And with that, came the nightmares—desperate people running. Panic. The staccato fire of an M-16.

And Lara—always, he saw Lara, her beautiful face broken and bleeding. He should've been able to drag her to safety before the second explosion. He could've saved her life.

But he'd been injured. Disoriented. And because he failed her, she died on a rocky, desolate road outside of Bagdad, her eyes filled with terror and his name on her lips…

Something damp and cool probed at his hand.

Opening his eyes, he found himself looking into the warm, sympathetic face of Elvis—the Border collie that followed Gus everywhere. The dog nudged his hand again and whined.

Josh swallowed hard and shoved away the images of violence that still plagued him, absurdly thankful for the dog's presence. "Did you get left behind too, sport?"

But Elvis didn't lean into him for attention. He shoved his nose under Josh's wrist and bumped it, hard—then he jumped off the porch and loped a few yards away before stopping and looking over his shoulder.

Exactly how some dog in a kids' movie would telegraph a call for help, only those things didn't happen in real life. Maybe he just wanted to play catch.

Elvis came back in a flash and stood just out of reach—then started to bark, the volume increasing exponentially until he was bouncing on his front feet with each effort.

"Okay, okay," Josh muttered. "I'll take your word for it. But this better be good."

He painstakingly limped inside to retrieve his other crutch, then awkwardly eased down the three porch steps, praying that he wouldn't fall flat on his face. Elvis ran ahead and came back a dozen times, each circuit taking him to the wide open door of the barn, while Josh made his way across the parking area.

By the time he made it to the door, he knew the dog's agitation was for real. And the second he stepped into cool shadows of the building, he knew way.

Halfway down the aisle, Gus was sprawled on the concrete, face down.

And he wasn't moving.

"I swear, she's gone—and so's the old lady. I saw them both leave. We gotta get movin' while we can." The man hung back in the shadows of the tall pines near the house. "You in, or are you out?"

"What about the old guy? What if *he's* in there?"

"He don't go in the big house 'cept to eat, and it ain't dinnertime. He and the old lady live in the east end of the bunkhouse. He's probably nappin', with the boss gone."

The smaller man fidgeted. "But what if—"

"Have I been wrong yet?"

"And that new guy—the one on crutches. What if—"

"You think I can't take out someone on *crutches?*

Anyways he hasn't come outside in two days, far as I can tell."

"Maybe we oughta move to that side of the house—so we can keep an eye out for him."

"And risk being seen? What are you, stupid?" Swearing under his breath, the bigger man crouched down and reached behind him to adjust the gun and holster hidden at the small of his back. "We'll be in and out in three minutes, tops. Now *shut up*."

Swiftly scanning the clearing, he ran to the back of the house, tested the screen door, then pulled out a knife and sliced the screen. He reached inside and unlocked the door.

Listened.

Then moved inside, with his companion right behind him. "You know what we gotta do. Right?"

Without looking over his shoulder, the bigger man crept into the depths of the house until he found the first floor office. Signaling his buddy, he then tore into the desk. The file drawers. Checked behind the pictures on the wall.

He found what he needed in the depths of a closet, behind a stack of boxes. "Got it," he said. "Now let's get outta here—"

They both froze.

The faint, discordant sound of sirens drifted through the house—and they were coming *closer.*

"You said there wasn't no security in this place," the shorter man snarled. "Guess you ain't so smart after all."

"Really?" Reaching for the holster at his back, the tall one debated. Then he dropped his hand and turned away. *Later, my friend. Later.*

He took a last look around and savored a surge of victory. Of vindication.

And then he followed his buddy out of the house at a dead run.

EIGHT

Josh had trained as an EMT during college, some-thing that had come in handy more than once during his years as a photojournalist in war-torn countries in the Middle East.

But that training had been almost fifteen years ago, he'd only kept up on CPR since then, and he'd certainly never tried to provide emergency medical care with an awkward cast on his leg and thirty sutures on his own belly.

By the time the ambulance and patrol cars arrived, Gus was still unconscious and his heart beat was erratic, but at least he was breathing.

Now, in the starkly lit emergency room of the tiny Wolf Creek Hospital—a place that was becom-ing entirely too familiar—he looked up at the sound of hurried footsteps and saw Tessa come around the corner, followed by an older woman with short-cropped silver hair.

Tessa's eyes widened at the sight of him, and he could've sworn that he caught a flash of fear in her expression. She hesitated, then set her jaw and dropped into the seat next to him. "How is Gus? Is—is he all right?"

"They can't really tell me anything. I'm not family. But Sofia got here a few minutes ago, and she's with him right now. If a nurse comes by, maybe you can send a message back there."

"How did you get here?"

"I…" He ducked his head. "Sort of borrowed Gus's truck."

"You drove? In that cast?"

"Lucky for me, it's on my left leg, and the truck has an automatic transmission. I figured I'd better follow the ambulance, so someone would be here for him until his wife came."

"Who is this, Tessa?" The older woman's voice was sharp, suspicious. "And why is he here?"

Tessa drew in a slow breath. "Claire, this is…Josh Bryant. He's a guest out at the ranch. And Josh, this is my mother, Claire McAllister."

Claire's gaze dropped pointedly to Josh's leg. "He certainly can't be going on any pack trips like that."

Tessa's shoulders relaxed, almost imperceptibly. "He was in an accident not far from the ranch, so he just needed a place to recuperate for a while. We put him in Ray's old cabin."

"Humph." The woman took a chair on the opposite side of the room, her narrowed eyes never leaving Josh's face. "There's something familiar about you."

"Well," Tessa exclaimed. "Does anyone need some coffee? Soda?"

Josh shifted in his chair, retrieved his billfold from the back pocket of his jeans, and pulled out a five. "It's on me, if you don't mind getting me a Coke."

She wavered, glancing between him and her mother, as if uncertain about whether or not she could leave them alone together.

"I understand Gus has worked for you a long time," he ventured after Tessa disappeared down the hall.

"Over forty years." Claire fixed him with a piercing look, as if trying to read his thoughts. "Where are you from?"

"Born in Texas, but I spent most of my years out East."

"Doing what?"

"Photographer, mostly. Scenic stuff, these days. Travel and nature magazines, human interest topics."

She frowned, clearly searching for some memory of him. But he knew they'd never met, and Tessa had certainly skirted the fact that she'd known him back in college. Why?

"Good thing you were around to help Gus," she said finally, settling back in her chair. "Couldn't have been easy with that leg of yours."

Tessa appeared with a Coke and two coffees, and glanced between them, her face pale. "Any word yet?"

"Stupid system," Claire muttered. "Gus is like a brother to me. Those fool doctors ought to be able to come out and tell us something."

A few minutes later, Sofia came through the double doors leading back to the ER, her eyes red and a crumpled tissue clutched in one hand. Her stride faltered when she looked between Claire and Josh, then she walked into Tessa's welcoming embrace.

"Tell us," Tessa whispered. "Is he all right?"

"H-heart attack."

"Is he—"

"They just ran more tests. They already gave him a drug to break the clot, and they've had to defibrillate him twice since he got here. I-I'm waiting to talk to the doctor."

Tessa guided Sofia to a chair and sat down next to her, still holding her hand. "I've been praying for him, and for you."

"And I haven't stopped praying since I got the call." Sofia gave Josh a watery smile. "How did you find my cell phone number?"

"It was on the tack room bulletin board, in the barn."

"The doctors say you saved my husband's life." She reached out to grasp his hand between both of hers. "If there's ever *anything* I can do for you, just say the word. I can't ever express how thankful I am."

"The EMTs are the ones who really did their job right." Josh started to rise, then drew in a sharp breath at a sudden stab of pain. Wobbled.

Tessa was across the room in a flash, grabbing his arm. She pushed him back into his chair. "Sit. Don't move. Understand?"

"I'm fine, Tess—"

"No, you're not. Sofia?"

The other woman hurried over to stand next to him, while Tessa disappeared through the double doors of the ER, calling for a nurse.

And it was only then that he looked down—and found his shirt was soaked in blood.

It was after midnight by the time Tessa dropped her mother off at Janna's place and got Josh back to his cabin.

"I couldn't be more thankful about you helping Gus the way you did," she said as she bustled around, pulling shades and turning on lamps. "But you remember what the doctor said, right? No heavy lifting. Take it *really* easy. Frankly, he seemed surprised that anyone could tear open his sutures like that. You must've worked on Gus with CPR for a long time."

"I really didn't have much choice." He gave her a weary smile. "And I'd do it all over again in a minute."

"I know." She hovered as he made his way across the room to the couch, then reached for his crutches when he set them aside. "And I'm thankful."

Their fingertips brushed, just a brief contact, but she felt her cheeks heat and she quickly turned away, embarrassed at her reaction.

"So now—" Her voice sounded breathless even to her own ears, and she swallowed hard. "Now, you need to take good care of yourself or that incision isn't going to heal. They said you were really lucky that you didn't do any internal damage."

"Tess." His voice was low, husky. Gently mocking. "I can take care of myself, but you probably need to get up to the house and get some sleep. It's been a long day for you, too."

"Right." She'd always been attracted to his dark, good looks. His intelligence and his sense of humor. But now, after what he'd done for Gus despite his own injuries, she felt more drawn to him than ever.

She backed toward the door, then turned and let herself out into the dark night.

She'd loved the solitude here…the complete absence of city lights, the blanket of stars at night. The discordant chorus of coyotes that filled the silence. It had always been exactly right, being here with just Gus and Sofia tucked in their private lodgings, and no one else to get in the way.

But now, as she walked to the house and let herself in the front door, she felt oddly lonely. Bereft. From the shock of nearly losing her old friend, probably.

But Sofia was most likely already on her way back to the ranch by now, as Gus had stabilized, and he'd insisted that she go home for a decent night's sleep. He would be home soon, too—the doctor had predicted that he'd have a four or five day stay in the hospital, and then up to thirty days in cardiac rehab at a skilled care center after that.

Thank you, Lord, for your mercy. For the life of my friend. For keeping him with us. Please, let him recover well and be strong, so he can enjoy retirement…

Locking the front door, she headed on through the

house to the back hall leading to her office and two main floor bedrooms, then took a detour to the kitchen to lock that door as well. Until the string of cabin break-ins in the area, she'd rarely locked up at night. But now—

She cocked her head, studying the back door, then fumbled for a light switch.

The heavy oak door was open, as usual, but the screen door was wide open, too. The screen itself was torn from top to bottom, and hung limp and useless.

She blinked, not believing what she saw, then moved closer.

This didn't appear to be the work of a raccoon trying to come in after food, or a larger animal that might've blundered into it. The screen looked as if it had been cut by a laser-sharp knife.

Her pulse stumbled as she spun on her heel, scanning the kitchen. Nothing was out of place. Not the pretty little potted ivy that still sat dead center on the round oak claw-foot table.

Not the neat stack of mail on the counter, or the orderly row of boots by the door. Even the cookie jar was untouched— a prime target for 'coons—and the old fishbowl by the phone was still full of the coins she tossed in whenever emptying her pockets before doing laundry.

Still scanning the room, she backed over to the entryway closet and retrieved Claire's old shotgun and a box of shells from the locked gun cabinet inside. Stood quiet and still for several long minutes, listening for sounds in the house.

The house felt empty—with that hollow, vacant aura of total silence. She wavered about calling the sheriff's office, then started a slow, methodical search of the main floor, flipping on the lights in the dining and living room as she went, then the hallway and bedroom lights.

Everything was pristine…the bedding neatly draped, the dresser drawers closed. No sign of someone pawing through her possessions in search of jewelry.

Calmer now, she reached the door to her office. She kept no cash here. All important documents were kept in a safe deposit box at the bank. So what could anyone find? Old receipts and livestock records, mostly. Anything more sensitive was safely filed away or shredded.

She flipped on the light, drew in a sharp breath, then jerked her cell phone from its case and tried to speed dial with shaking fingers. After two false starts, she managed to make the call, then leaned against the door frame and fought back her rising nausea.

Desk drawers hung askew. Boxes had been pulled out of the closet and thrown across the room. And covering every flat surface was a blizzard of papers that had once been neatly filed.

Someone had been here, but he—or she—hadn't grabbed the heirloom jewelry in her dresser. The twenties laying on her bureau. The Nikon camera that still sat on top of one of the file cabinets.

So what on earth had they been after?

Lost in thought, she sorted through the wreckage, feeling violated and angry—

And then, she heard footsteps coming down the hall.

NINE

Tessa stilled at the sound of heavy footsteps coming down the hall toward her office. She moved farther into the room, easing her right hand to the trigger of her shotgun. "Who's there?" she called out.

The steps drew closer. "Only me, Tess."

At hearing Josh's deep voice, an uncomfortable mix of relief and anger rushed through her. "What are you doing here?" she demanded. "And how did you get in?"

"The back door was open. You need to fix that screen one of these days, by the way." He appeared at her office door, propped up with one crutch, his face weary. "I saw all the lights, and thought maybe something had happened to Gus, so— Good grief, what happened in here?"

"I—I don't know." She waved a hand at the litter. "While I was gone, someone tore into my files and went through storage boxes. My computer's external back-up drive is missing. When I tried turning on the computer, it started to sizzle and smoke, so they did something to it, too. Michael ought to be here any minute. When I called, he was just a few miles away."

Josh hobbled into the room to survey the damage, his face grim. "I'm just thankful you weren't here. Any idea what someone could be after?"

"Not a clue. Maybe money, but they left a couple hundred dollars in silver change in the bowl on the kitchen counter, and they didn't take an expensive camera."

A moment later, a knock sounded at the back door, and Michael walked in to join them, carrying a slender case. With a perfunctory nod at Josh, he gave Tessa a quick hug, then he stepped back, still gently holding her hands.

"Your sisters are going to worry when they hear about this," he said. "After that gunshot wound, Janna wanted you to bring in a security system and a pit bull."

"When you go home, tell her I'm fine. Do you think this is tied in to those cabin break-ins?"

He scanned the room. "What's missing?"

"Other than an external backup for the computer, nothing that I can see. They walked right by valuables, but made a mess in here."

"Then this would be a complete departure from the previous break-ins. Those thieves have gone solely after high tech, big ticket items—plasma screen TVs and the like. Or jewelry."

"Maybe this was an attempt at identity theft— or a hunt for bank or investment account numbers," Josh said.

"A lot of that happens through Internet and e-mail schemes these days, or with thefts from mailboxes, but this seems a lot more focused and personal." Michael donned a pair of latex gloves and pulled some plastic bags from his briefcase, then began picking up random sheets of paper that had been scattered across the room. "With luck, your friends weren't smart enough to wear gloves, and their prints are already in IAFIS."

"What?"

"The nationwide database for fingerprints."

"That would be just too easy," Tessa said, dropping into her desk chair. "How long does it take to find out?"

"Jackson County doesn't have its own crime lab. They have to be sent on to a latent print examiner in the next county, then go via a terminal to the state lab—then the FBI."

"So we won't know tomorrow."

Michael shook his head. "A case like this one won't take high priority. We might not hear for weeks."

"In other words, someone has to die for them to care?"

"They care. They just don't have the manpower." Michael dropped the evidence bags into his case, then pulled out his clipboard and began jotting notes. "I'd definitely contact one of the three main credit bureaus to request a fraud alert, and you'd better contact your bank, too."

He wrote a few notes, then looked up at Tessa. "Where were you this afternoon and evening?"

"I was with my mother until around six. I was on my way to take her home when I heard about Gus, so we went straight to the hospital."

"How about you, Josh?"

"I was here, until Elvis insisted that something was wrong." At Michael's raised eyebrow, Josh added, "The dog just wouldn't leave me alone, and kept running between me and the barn. I found Gus on the floor out there, then I followed the ambulance into town and stayed in the waiting room."

"Tell me again about what brought you out to Wyoming."

"A photo assignment. Though I've made zero progress on it, and time is flying."

Michael smiled. "I've always wondered how that works. Are you salaried?"

"If you're asking whether or not I'm strapped financially, the answer is no. And there's no way I'd ever steal from a friend or anyone else."

Michael met his gaze for a long, unwavering moment, then turned to Tessa. "What about Danny?"

"No matter what anyone says, he's a good kid," Tessa retorted. "Everyone around here wants to make him guilty by association, and that's just plain wrong."

"No one's saying he's guilty of anything. I just want to know where he was."

"Working, so he *wasn't* with his old buddies. He came up mid-afternoon to get things ready for one of our trail rides with a campfire supper. He would've been back with the clients around nine o'clock."

"And what time did you get back?"

"After midnight. I dropped Josh at his place, then came to the house and discovered the ripped screen."

"And you walked right in anyway." Michael frowned at her. "Not a good idea, Tess. You should've called 911 and waited. What if you'd surprised someone?"

"I had a shotgun."

He shook his head slowly. "You and your sisters are too independent for your own good. One of these days, you're going to walk into a situation that you *can't* handle…and then I'll just be praying that I can get to you in time."

"I can handle myself."

"Can you?" He rested a hand on her shoulder. "We've never figured out who fired that shot at you. Was it accidental—or on purpose? Was it intentionally just a graze, or was that guy trying for center mass? There've been two other break-ins in the county, and so far, no one has been hurt. But whether the incidents are related or not, you've been a target twice."

With Gus in the hospital, Sofia headed into town early the next morning, and Josh knew she'd likely stay there late. Tessa's truck left the ranch a few minutes later and by mid-morning, Danny had left with a trio of fly fishermen for a three-day weekend pack trip.

Since her only hired hand was out of commission, Josh could guess at how overwhelmed Tessa must be, dealing with livestock and her outfitting clients.

He scowled at the cast on his leg. Nine days down and eternity to go. His leg didn't hurt any longer, but the inconvenience had driven his frustration level to the limit. How could he sit around doing nothing, when everyone was dealing with so much?

From across the room came a tinny version of Liszt's "Hungarian Rhapsody No. 2," courtesy of his cell phone. Leaving his crutches behind, he limped over to the counter.

"Where have you *been?*" The impatient voice of Sylvia Meiers, his editor, burst out of the phone before he could even say hello. We haven't heard from you in three weeks!"

"Wyoming, as planned." He eyed his cast in disgust. "Though I did run into a little difficulty."

"I don't want to hear about your 'difficulties,' Josh. I want to hear that this time, you'll be e-mailing me your article and photos with time to spare."

Her sharp voice felt like a stiletto driving into his ear. But the words she *didn't* say—about articles he'd been unable to complete—rang in his ears nonetheless. And those words were even more painful, because they dredged up every memory he had of his years in the Middle East with *World Focus* magazine, and that terrible final day…

The job offer at *Green Earth*, a sister publication, had felt like a lifeline. A last chance to fulfill the only goal he cared about now.

But thanks to a speeding pickup and a narrow mountain road, he was going to fail once again.

"Did you find some ranchers who would cooperate?"

"Just as planned."

"Well…good." She definitely sounded suspicious. "You know, Josh, that I shouldn't have given you this assignment. Harv Franklin wanted you fired."

Her voice pulled him back to the present. "I've got it covered." *Liar, liar.*

"June 28th, Josh. I expect your e-mailed files no later than that. And no excuses, because I put my neck on the line for you. We've got the layout planned, and I need this material on time or I promise you, this will be the end of your career."

Something, he supposed, that she could accomplish with a few well-placed phone calls. The parent company of the magazine owned eight of the biggest selling periodicals in the country, and Sylvia's widespread connections in the industry were well-known.

But this would be his last assignment no matter what Sylvia did, and it wouldn't be for her sake that he finished it.

It would be for Lara's.

Long after Sylvia's call ended, Josh slowly paced the room, forcing himself to bear weight on his injured leg. Ignoring the increasing pain until he finally flopped on the sofa, defeated. Toughing out the discomfort just wasn't going to work.

The surgeon had said that the original cast would

stay on for at least six weeks, depending on how fast he healed. She'd promised to consider a walking cast in four.

But that simply wasn't good enough.

Josh could start his research on the Internet and begin writing the article. But he couldn't sit here—he had to get out to interview ranchers and hear their views on the environmental issues surrounding grazing rights on this fragile, arid land.

And he had to be mobile—so he could hike into the higher ranges, where livestock grazed on government allotments. And that would be impossible with his cast.

Unless…he glanced out the window toward the barn, where Danny had left a four-wheeler parked by the front door, and smiled, for the first time in days. Maybe he could even find a good way to thank Tessa for her hospitality, before he left Wyoming for good.

With Gus in the hospital, Tessa had set her alarm for five, finished chores, loaded a horse into her stock trailer and drove down to Wolf Creek to pick up calf supplement at the feed store when it opened at eight o'clock.

After stopping at the hospital to see Gus, she went to the bank to notify them of the possible theft of identity information and bank account numbers, then spent the rest of the day on horseback, checking on the ninety cow-calf pairs pastured up in the Arrow-head Valley, and the broodmares closer to home.

Back at the ranch, there were a couple of two-year-old colts to work and chores to do all over again, and the thought of rustling anything up for supper sounded even more exhausting…except, she'd told Josh that he wouldn't have to worry about cooking his own meals, and he certainly wouldn't have any groceries to work with. What on earth was she going to feed him?

With a long sigh, she trudged up the steps to the wide, covered porch of the main house. Pulled open the front door…

And detected what had to be the most wonderful aroma this side of heaven.

"Sofia?" She closed her eyes for a moment in sheer bliss, then headed down the hall to the kitchen. "I didn't think you'd be back this early—"

Josh turned away from the stove, a sheepish grin on his face. "I sorta let myself in. Hope you don't mind."

She glanced around the kitchen. "That's fine. Where's Sofia?"

"She'll be home in a half hour. She called my cell just a few minutes ago."

Surprised, Tessa took a closer look at him. "Y-you're *cooking?*"

He tipped his head toward the stove. "I knew you'd have a long day and that Sofia would be back late. It's the least I could do."

"'The least you could do'? It smells fantastic! What is it?"

He glanced ruefully at his cast, and the single crutch propped under his arm. "It was the easiest thing I could come up with. I found some steak in your freezer, and went from there. We're having steak au poivre—with a few recipe substitutions—mashed potatoes and honey-glazed baby carrots. I couldn't find the ingredients for much else, so it's nothing fancy."

Tessa's stomach growled. "Nothing *fancy?* It sounds wonderful."

He turned back to the cast-iron skillet on the stove and flipped over the steaks, then ladled on a sauce. "It's all ready, and you probably shouldn't wait for Sofia. I can take my plate out to my place…"

"Please, stay. I'll set the table for all three of us." While he tended the stove, she washed up, then set the dining-room table and filled the water glasses.

It wasn't until she came back into the kitchen that she noticed Elvis curled up contentedly at the end of the counter, his eyes riveted on Josh.

Josh followed her gaze and smiled. "I…couldn't help it. He was running all over, trying to find Gus, then he took a look at me and must've decided I was a good enough second-stringer. He's been my shadow ever since. He…um…didn't want to stay outside alone."

She didn't have to taste dinner to know it would be wonderful—the aromas were already out-of-this-world. The thoughtfulness of his effort was touching.

But a man who cooked, and who would befriend a lonely dog pining for its beloved owner? The combination was potent…and just like that, her heart melted.

And that was bad news.

It had been okay, having Josh here at the ranch. It had been the right and neighborly thing to do, and she'd managed to keep a cool distance that betrayed none of her old emotions.

But what was she going to do now?

TEN

Josh started with that incredible recipe for steak.

After that, he made something different every night, finding odds and ends in the freezer and pantry, and coming up with mouth-watering menus that had her looking forward to getting back home after a long day in the saddle.

Sofia, exhausted after her days at Gus's side in the hospital, had been dubious at first. And then she fell under Josh's spell, too, during her late-night, re-heated dinners back at the ranch—especially when he insisted that he'd like to make meals several times a week after her husband came home, so she'd have one less thing to worry about.

But soon things would go back to normal—almost.

Sofia had moved Gus from the hospital to a skilled care facility, and he would be there for a month. He'd probably be laid up at the ranch for weeks after that, and there still hadn't been any viable responses to Tessa's employment ads in the local newspaper.

She'd managed to cover the daily ranch work for

the past week by herself and Danny was handling all of the trail rides and trips, but now, Josh was asking for the four-wheeler keys so he could go sightseeing, which presented a new worry.

"You're *sure* you'll be okay?" She glanced down at his cast. "The quad isn't exactly new. What if you have engine problems and you're too far away to walk back?"

He grinned and dangled his cell phone by its little antenna. "I'll call."

"*If* you're in range. And I won't necessarily be in range, either, so I wouldn't go too far, if I were you."

He held up two fingers in a scout salute. "Promise."

"Do you know the boundaries of the ranch?" Without waiting for a response, she walked into the tack room in the barn, then returned with a brochure from her outfitting business and opened it up on the hood of her truck. "Here's a map. We have a little over a thousand acres. To the west, it's all government land—Kilbourne Creek marks that boundary."

"Got it."

"Four Winds Ranch is to the south—and that's owned by my sister Leigh's future husband, Cole Daniels. There's private land to the north, and beyond that, a condominium and resort complex, which is also private land. So going to the north is out. Obviously, the mountains are to the west, and that's mostly federal land."

"Understood." He frowned, and tapped the next ranch to the north. "So, what's that land used for?"

"Mostly cattle—same as Four Winds and Snow Canyon Ranch. In Iowa, it might take three or four acres to support a single cow, but here it takes a good thirty-five to forty. Our ranches have to be *huge*."

Josh's eyes twinkled and his dimples deepened. "That's just amazing, to an Easterner like me."

"Even so, we couldn't make it without our grazing leases on government land to stay afloat." She folded up the map and handed it to him. "Owning enough land would be impossible for most of the ranchers around here."

"I suppose the government has endless regulations, though."

"Of course, but it's in our interest to comply. We have to rotate pastures and limit the number of head per acre, because the land is so fragile. Ruin the land, and our ranching lifestyle is gone."

He whistled. "Have you thought about relocating?"

"This ranch is home, and I'll never leave," she said simply, tossing him the quad keys. "Now, be careful and don't get yourself lost or hurt, okay? And try to stay on the trails if you go up into the high country." She watched him climb aboard the vehicle by gingerly lifting his cast into position first. "You're bringing food and water?"

He shrugged his backpack into better position. "You bet."

"Rain gear? Weather changes fast, around here—especially up at the higher elevations."

"Got it." With a wave, he turned the ignition key

and sped across the barnyard in a cloud of dust, heading toward a pasture gate. "I'll be back before dark," he shouted over the noise of the engine.

She watched him go, amused by his exuberance over being free of the limitations of his crutches and cast…though another thought niggled at her.

He'd been friendly. Sociable. And as usual, she'd been totally disarmed by his lazy grin and that flirty twinkle in his eyes.

So why did she have the uneasy feeling that he'd been fishing for information, and that he had a hidden agenda for being here?

"How dare you bring that man here," Claire snarled, her white-knuckled grip on the back of a chair threatening to snap the wood in two. "Did you think I wouldn't remember the name?"

Tessa had been hoping, but she probably should've been *praying* on it.

She tipped her head toward the plate of burgundy beef stew and biscuits on the table. "Have some lunch. You haven't eaten since early this morning."

"You don't remember what he did? He abandoned you without a care in the world. Never looked back." Claire snorted in disgust. "Then he went off and enjoyed some fancy career and left you to—"

"Enough," Tessa said firmly. "I don't want to discuss it."

Claire huffed. "I'll bet you never told him. Not even now. What kind of—"

"*Mom.*" The common maternal endearment, one Claire had always disliked, had the effect of a splash of ice water, just as Tessa expected.

Claire glared at her, then snapped her mouth shut.

"Please, your food is getting cold. I'll sit down and eat with you, okay? It's absolutely delicious—even better warmed over from last night." And Josh had made it, though she certainly wouldn't mention that, or the plate might go flying against the wall.

Claire, caught between pride and the wonderful aromas of the meal, hesitated, then jerked the chair away from the table, its legs screeching against the floor.

She sat down, ramrod straight, and poked at the entrée with her fork as if expecting it to startle and take flight. "What did Sofia do to this beef?"

"The recipe makes a savory, rich glaze. It's really good." Tessa took her place across the table from Claire and served herself from the stoneware baking dish sitting in the middle of the table. She took a bite, closing her eyes to concentrate on the explosion of flavor on her tongue.

"And where is she?" Claire demanded.

"Gus had a heart attack, remember? She's been spending a lot of time with him at the care center, helping with his therapy."

A flash of confusion crossed Claire's face, then cleared. Like a bloodhound, she picked up her target scent again. "Don't you think it's a little ironic that Josh Bryant would end up at your ranch?"

Tessa coughed on a forkful of parsley-buttered new potatoes. "You think he engineered a plan to stay here? No one would purposely risk an accident like his. He was nearly killed, and he needed *surgery.*"

"But he was *here.* In the area."

"Why would it have anything to do with me? I haven't heard from him since college." Tessa took a long sip of sweet tea. "And it's obvious that we aren't wealthy, if you think he's after money."

"It's too coincidental."

"That's all it is, Claire. A coincidence." But she couldn't quite meet her mother's eyes.

"He said he's a photographer," Claire snapped. "So what's he after?"

"I doubt it's anything *sinister.*"

"Are you really that naive?"

Tessa silently counted to ten. "The first time I saw him, he said he'd come to Wyoming for a photo shoot, and he was taking pictures of plants along a trail. That doesn't sound like any big secret to me."

"But isn't that how those tree huggers work?" Claire sniffed. "Don't forget that commotion over grazing rights on BLM government land last year. Those photos hit the papers clear to Billings and Denver."

"I'll talk to him, okay? Would that help?"

"Think what you will, but that Josh is a no-good, manipulative, self-centered, irresponsible—"

"Mom!" Tessa clenched her hands in her lap, biting back the words she'd regret.

"You know better than to call me that, young lady. I'll have some *respect*."

It wasn't a request. It wasn't framed with a please or thank you. And to most mothers, "mom" was hardly a derogatory term. But then, Janna had said she was noticing an increase in Claire's outbursts lately, as well as increasing forgetfulness and confusion. Added to her imperious nature, the progress of her dementia was becoming even more challenging.

"I hear you're going to town for a doctor's appointment on Friday," Tessa said, trying for a breezy tone. "That's good."

"It's a waste of time. I'm not going." Claire dug into her lunch, polishing off the last morsel before looking up again. "Already take too much medicine as it is—and that's a waste of good money. Doesn't work, anyhow."

Janna had made the appointment in hopes that a change in medication would help, but no one could deny Claire's grim future—especially since she refused to take her medicine half the time.

The back door squealed open and Sofia charged up the three steps into the kitchen, her face damp with perspiration.

"I think you need to call your sister Leigh right away," she exclaimed, breathing hard. She nodded a greeting at Claire, then she turned back to Tessa with an expression of distress and lowered her voice. "It's your mother's horse, Socks. I found her loose in the barn, with the feed room door open. I don't know how full that sack of calf supplement was, but it's all gone now…and that horse sure doesn't look right."

"What was that?" Claire barked. "Something about my horse?"

Tessa grabbed her cell phone and ran for the back door. "I'll go check it out, Mom," she called out. "You stay here with Sofia."

By the time Leigh pulled up in her vet truck, Tessa had tugged and coaxed the mare out of the barn, and had her front hooves planted in a couple of low, black rubber tubs filled with cool water. Tessa held the lead rope in one hand and a slowly running water hose in the other, to keep the water cool and circulating.

Despite her instructions to the contrary, Claire had followed Tessa to the barn, and now she and Sofia were standing to one side. But for once, Claire was silent. Watching. Her face was a mask of worry.

"Just the front hooves were hot, Leigh. It must have taken me ten minutes to get her out here. She was in a lot of pain." Tessa tossed the end of the hose into a stock tank on the other side of the fence.

Leigh pulled her long, strawberry blond ponytail through the back of her ball cap and frowned at the mare's stance.

No wonder. Already, Socks had adopted the typical stance of acute laminitis, with her front legs extended to relieve the intense pain and pressure inside the unyielding outer walls of her hooves.

"How long would you say it's been since she got in the feed?"

"Everything was fine this morning when I did chores." Tessa reached out to stroke the mare's sweaty neck. "I always double-latch the feed room door, and I double check it before I leave. And I always check the stall doors, too. Everything was fine before I left for the Lodge to get Claire. But when we got back here, I didn't go to the barn—it was lunchtime, so we went straight to the house."

Leigh jogged into the barn and looked into the feed room, then came back outside. "How full was that bag of calf supplement?"

"I hadn't opened it yet. It was a twenty-five pound bag."

"Has she been rolling or showing any signs of colic?"

"Nope—thank goodness."

"Did you give her any medications yet?"

"I thought about it, but you said you could get here right away, so I thought I better leave everything up to you." Tessa managed a small smile. "You're the expert, after all."

Leigh darted a glance at Claire, clearly waiting for a sarcastic remark and surprised that their mother didn't offer one. "I'll do my best for your mare. I hope we've gotten to her in time to minimize any permanent damage."

She bent over and lifted one hoof and then the other, moving aside the water tubs and first holding the hoof between her hands to check for heat, then palpating for the digital pulse just above each hoof, at the back.

With a grim expression, she jogged back to her vet truck and retrieved syringes and small bottles, then came back and drew up three syringes of medication that she handed to Tessa.

After palpating the mare's neck and finding the right vein, she delivered the medications slowly, one after another.

"I've given her Bute, which is an anti-inflammatory, and some DMSO. I also gave her a vasodilator to increase her blood flow. She's going to be feeling a lot better soon, but she needs to be on deep, soft bedding in her stall." Leigh frowned. "Keep her on stall rest, and you can continue to give her Bute for the pain if she needs it. Give it to her in the muscle, though."

"She's going to be okay?" Claire asked.

Her voice was so soft and shaky that all three women turned to look at her in concern.

"Leigh has done everything right," Tessa said. "She's gaining quite a reputation in these parts."

Claire moved closer and rested a hand on the mare's nose. "Socks is an old gal. I'm not sure how well she'll come through something like this."

"I'll do X-rays tomorrow, and then come back a few days later and check her again," Leigh said, handing the bottle of Bute to Tessa. "If she still isn't doing well, we'll need to look at other measures."

Claire nodded, then rested her forehead against

the mare's cheek. "Thank you, Leigh. I—I'm not sure I ever said it, but I'm proud of what you've done, being a vet, and all."

Obviously taken aback, Leigh looked up and met Tessa's eyes before reaching out to briefly touch their mother's arm. "Thanks."

Surprised at Claire's brief display of affection, Tessa stepped away and hurried down the aisle of the barn to prepare a stall for the mare by tossing in two extra bales of sawdust and fluffing it with a pitchfork.

After the mare was back in her stall, Sofia took Claire down to her cabin for a cup of coffee, but Tessa lingered in the barn with Leigh.

"Do you really think Socks will be okay?"

"I hope so—for Claire's sake. She loves that old mare like one of her kids."

"Or more so." Tessa gave a rueful laugh. "The sad thing is that it's taken old age for her to allow even a glimpse of her softer side. Do you ever what she would've been like, if Dad hadn't died so young?"

"I don't even remember him." Leigh's expression turned wistful. "Do you?"

"Barely. Hearing him laugh, I guess. Otherwise, I'm not sure which memories are real, and which stem from what someone else said. I know…well, that they didn't have the happiest marriage."

Leigh rolled her eyes. "Can you imagine our mother ever giving an inch on *anything?*"

"The McAllisters don't have a great history of

marital success, but Janna and Michael sure seem solid. And if anyone can succeed, it'll be you and Cole. That man *adores* you."

"I just want to make it past the wedding. I've had almost no time to work on it, and it's less than four weeks away."

The cell phone at her hip rang, and she answered quickly, then pulled a notepad from the back pocket of her coveralls and wrote something down.

"I have to go," she said as soon as she hung up and jammed the phone back in its holster. "A horse ran through a fence and has some severe lacerations. I'll come back tomorrow to check on Socks."

She started toward her truck, then turned back. "I heard over the scanner that another batch of wildfires has started about five miles from town. Deliberately set, according to the fire crews."

"That's what I heard, too. Who could be that crazy? This whole area could go up in smoke."

Leigh nodded. "And I keep wondering if a single person is behind all of this…and if it's the same guy who's been harassing you. Be careful, Tess. You could still be in danger."

ELEVEN

Leigh's words replayed through Tessa's thoughts long after her sister left on the vet call, and during the long drive back to Snow Canyon Lodge, when Tessa took their mother home.

Clearly tired after her day at the ranch, Claire headed straight inside to her bedroom, but Janna came out to visit. Michael pulled in just minutes later.

"Glad to see you, Tess," he said as he climbed out of his patrol car and strolled over to Tessa's truck. "I've got news...sort of."

She smiled. "I hope it's good."

"I called in a favor at the state crime lab, and have an answer on that evidence from your burglary. The only identifiable prints were from you or your mother."

Disappointment washed through her. "So the intruder wore gloves, then."

"Probably."

"And I didn't find anything at all when I cleaned up that mess. Would've been awfully nice to find some really obvious clue." Feeling defeated, she sighed.

"Maybe it was just a random, one-time deal. Someone who thought the McAllisters keep piles of money sitting around, and found that he'd totally wasted his time."

A corner of Michael's mouth lifted. "You wouldn't' believe how many people make that assumption. They give me a sly grin and wink, if my marriage to Janna comes up."

Janna grinned and bumped him with her elbow. "Maybe you'll have that kind of success, once this resort takes off."

"It should. Your Web site is beautiful, and this has to be the prettiest place on the planet." Tessa turned to Michael. "Leigh tells me the most recent wildfires were probably set. Is that true?"

"They weren't ignited by lightning. But whether they were set intentionally or started by careless campers, we don't know yet."

Tessa shivered. "This whole area is tinder-dry. If there's enough wind and the wrong location, it could be devastating."

"We're already evacuating homes and campgrounds west of Shawnee Creek. That one started on private land and spread into the national forest within hours. Over five hundred acres are gone already. It could be in the thousands by daybreak, if the incident management team can't contain it."

"Are you seeing any pattern?" Janna wrapped her arms around her middle.

"The last three have started close to some luxury

cabins that were burgled." He looked over his shoulder toward the towering mountains forming the western horizon. "Two fires were discovered by deputies responding to security system alarms. I hear the fire season hasn't started this early in years."

With the breeze coming from the west, the air was hazy and acrid with smoke, and Tessa's eyes burned. "Guess I'd better go. I still have evening chores, and I should get into town and visit Gus."

Michael shot a quick glance at Janna, nodded, then touched Tessa's shoulder. "We'd be happy to welcome you, Gus and Sofia over here, if you'd feel safer. Your friend, too."

Surprised, Tessa laughed, sure that it had been Janna's idea. A warm feeling curled around her heart at the relationships with her sisters that were deepening after far too many years of estrangement. "That's nice of you, but we're good. All of my work is over there, and I'd spend hours commuting. Thanks, anyway."

"Both of us are concerned, Tess," Janna looped an arm through the crook of Michael's elbow. "I just keep thinking about the day someone shot at you. Maybe he's the one breaking into the cabins, and is afraid you saw too much. So he tore up your office as sort of a warning."

Tessa smiled. "You do have a good imagination. This is little Wolf Creek, Wyoming, not some drama on TV."

"No, it's not," Janna said urgently. "It's *scary*. I

agree with Leigh—this is all connected somehow, and I think the guy is escalating. And someone is going to get hurt."

Josh was an adequate rider, though he hadn't grown up on horseback like the McAllisters. But one glance at the pack horses kept in a small pasture by Tessa's barn, and he knew they were in serious trouble.

He parked the four-wheeler and studied the animals through the fence.

It was late afternoon, and they looked drowsy, like they usually did on warm summer afternoons. They were probably still tired from their long pack trip over the weekend. But two of the five horses were moving oddly, with a random, stumbling gait.

One of them made its way to the water tank, where it plunged its muzzle into the water, obviously thirsty but not coordinating well enough to drink. The other one seemed to be mouthing something, its lips twitching and tongue flicking in and out. The motion reminded him of a dog when given a piece of a peanut butter sandwich that was sticking to the roof of its mouth.

The two mules, however, looked perfectly content and were eating at a pile of something fresh and green at the farthest end of the corral.

He called Tessa's cell phone. No answer, but he left a message.

Then he limped over to Gus and Sofia's cabin, but she was gone—probably at the care center once again.

After trying the phone number at Snow Canyon Lodge, he went back to the corral and watched the horses for a while longer.

None of them seemed to be in pain, exactly, and they had plenty of water, shade, and a nice pile of green…whatever, at the far end of the corral, so they had plenty to eat.

He debated, then tried Tessa's phone once more before calling Leigh for her veterinary opinion. Would Tessa resent his presumption in calling a vet? So be it—those horses didn't look right, and losing any of them would be a big blow to her business.

Leigh called him back in ten minutes. She fired off a series of questions and seemed strangely interested in the fact that the mules were fine and happily munching the pile of greenery in their pen while only the horses appeared to be affected.

With urgent orders for him to remove all of the feed immediately, she promised to reach the ranch within an hour or two—as soon as she finished emergency surgery on a llama.

After driving the four-wheeler to the far side of the corral to take the food away from the mules, Josh parked in the shade near the corral, slid his backpack-style camera bag from his shoulders, and lifted out his Canon EOS-5D.

It still felt light and unfamiliar in his hands, after years of working with his rugged old favorite, but it offered triple the megapixels and far better image quality. And once he'd started shooting photos of the drought conditions here, he'd begun envisioning the creation of a coffee-table book focusing on the wild beauty of this land.

He limped over to the fence and snapped off a few dozen frames of the mules, their heads low and long ears flopping over as they dozed. The two horses looked even worse than they had before.

It was clear that Tessa was operating on a shoestring here. He had no idea what a good pack horse might cost, but losing the entire string would have to be bad news for her business, and lead to expensive cancellations.

He glanced at his watch, then made his way back to the four-wheeler and climbed on, propping his cast on a fender.

For the past week, he'd been taking the little vehicle on fact-finding trips. Snapping hundreds of photographs of government land and cattle. The deep trails the animals carved across the fragile land where the soil was desperately thin and the grass sparse.

He'd made a couple of trips to town as well—by borrowing the ranch truck with the automatic transmission, so he could manage with one foot, then leaving a couple of twenties on Tessa's kitchen counter in repayment, each time he went.

Surprising, how approachable people were after he'd awkwardly navigated through the doors of a café and settled down at a table for coffee and the local newspaper.

When they learned that he wanted to write a

series of articles on the West, they invariably settled in for long conversations, and if they agreed to being quoted, he added those notes to his growing stack of files.

Sylvia expected him to let her down, but it wasn't going to happen. Not when he had so much at stake.

Except now…some of his preconceptions were changing, after talking with people whose lives were so deeply tied to the land, so greatly affected by hardships out of their control.

"Yellow star thistle," Leigh announced as she sifted through the pile of green vegetation that Josh had taken away from the mules. "It only affects horses—not mules or burros."

The plants looked like ordinary weeds to him, with a few tiny yellow flowers here and there. "So this is poisonous?"

"You bet, though it usually takes a month or two of ingesting it to show the worst signs. It causes a neurological disorder—a lot like Parkinson's in people."

Josh frowned, and glanced at the corral. "So you think these horses have had access to it for that long?"

"If they're showing significant symptoms, yes." She paced across the small pasture, studying the sparse vegetation, then returned. "But I don't see any of that weed growing out here. Every rancher knows it's bad and tries to eradicate it when they find some spreading onto their land."

"But these horses are kept close to the barn, so

they're handy for pack trips. They aren't out on the main pastures at all."

Leigh climbed over the fence and hunkered down next to the pile of yellow star thistle. She picked up a stem and studied it closely, then another. "I hoped that maybe there was just a random stand of this stuff growing at the end of the pasture—something natural. But these stems were cut, Josh. By something sharp—probably a scythe."

Their eyes met, and he instantly knew what she was thinking. "Someone went to a lot of work, you know that? Cutting all of this…secretly bringing it out here."

"Some horses develop a real taste for this stuff, and will choose it over good grass, crazy as that sounds. Maybe this guy figured it would always be eaten by morning so no one would be the wiser. And it worked, until you noticed something today."

"So how much would a horse have to eat?"

She glanced over her shoulder at the two horses that looked the most ill. "Someone must've been here a number of times. What I don't understand is *why.* I mean, if he wanted to cause trouble, why wouldn't he just shoot the horses and be done with it?"

"Too obvious," Josh said decisively. "The sheriff would be called right away. But something more natural…well, animals get sick, they die. So what's the prognosis?"

"Not good. We're dealing with a neurotoxin, and there really isn't an effective treatment with this one. With rest and time…well, hopefully, they'll come out of it, since they won't be eating any more of that plant. But there's no guarantee, and sometimes euthanasia is the only option."

"So they won't be usable for some time?"

"If ever." She turned to leave. "I'll bring my dog over a little later. Elvis is a sweetheart, but he'd rather welcome a thief than bark at him. Hobo is a *serious* watch dog."

"He won't just skedaddle for home?"

"I'll set up a wireless transmitter for an electric dog fence, and he'll wear a radio collar, so he'll stay within the vicinity of the barns and corrals. Believe me, he'll let you know if anyone shows up." She glanced at her watch. "I've got to get going, but I'll call Michael and tell him about this on the way to my next stop."

Josh watched her leave, then he turned back to the horses. What kind of person would purposely poison such beautiful animals and make them suffer?

It didn't take long to come up with some answers.

This wasn't just random malice. It had taken time, and effort, and planning. It was personal, and it was directed at Tessa.

Without her string of pack horses, her business would flounder. Replacing them would be an expensive and lengthy process, and in the meantime, she'd have to cancel scheduled trips and would probably lose some of those customers for good.

So who would profit most if that happened?

TWELVE

Tessa had been out checking on her cattle—something she was doing several times a week now, given that ten head were still missing—and had been out of reception range.

But the minute Tessa got back to her truck, loaded Dusty into the horse trailer, and climbed behind the wheel, she checked her messages.

There were three from clients, asking about upcoming pack trips into the mountains. Two from Danny, who said he wasn't feeling well and wouldn't be coming in today or tomorrow to help with the either of the scheduled half-day rides. One from Kirby Fellows from the feed store, with a disturbing comment about Josh...something that she would need to start watching.

And then there was the message from Josh himself.

She listened to it twice, then snapped her phone shut, turned on the ignition and headed back to the home place, her anger and frustration growing with every mile.

It wasn't fair. It just wasn't fair.

Some of the people in these parts had good reason to hold a grudge, given Claire's iron will and ruthlessness in business dealings, but Tessa couldn't undo the past anymore than she could stop the sun from setting. She'd done nothing but work hard and try to deal honestly with everyone in this town.

Yet old feelings died hard, and some people refused to forgive and forget. And someone seemed determined to see the McAllisters pay dearly for whatever harm they'd caused in the past. There certainly wasn't a lack of possibilities on that score.

Until now, Tessa had wanted to believe that her minor gunshot wound was an accident, and the break-in at her house was just a random incident—probably by the person who'd been burglarizing cabins in the area. But this—an attempt to destroy her pack string and ruin her business—put everything into perspective.

Just as Janna had said, someone was after her, and this person was escalating. Were they responsible for the theft of her cattle as well? And how could she ever figure out who this elusive, faceless person was, who seemed to be craftily assaulting her life from different angles?

It would be like trying to capture the wind.

After unloading Dusty and unhitching the trailer, Tessa strode over to the pasture she used for the pack horses and slipped inside.

The two mules and three of the horses looked up at her with mild curiosity and then kept grazing. But the other two horses stood together at the far end of the pasture, and even from a distance she could see something was wrong.

Both of them appeared dazed and were displaying the usual signs of star thistle poisoning—the twitching of their lips and the odd chewing motion. It was rare, now that ranchers were aware of the danger. But Tessa had seen the strange syndrome as a child, and she'd never forgotten it.

On her way into the barn, she speed dialed Leigh, but only reached her voice mail. Then she called Michael and had to leave a message on his cell phone when he didn't answer, either.

At least Socks seemed to be doing well. The old mare nickered softly when Tessa appeared at the front of her stall, and she moved without significant lameness to press her muzzle against the bars for a quick scratch.

"How is she?"

Josh's voice echoed down the long, dark aisle, and Tessa looked up to see him silhouetted against the bright, early evening sunshine. "Better. I'm just hoping we caught her in time, so she doesn't have permanent damage."

He came down the aisle, his one crutch and the cast giving him an uneven gait. Despite Kirby's troubling message, she still felt a little thrill of awareness when he stopped and looked down at her, his thickly lashed hazel eyes filled with compassion.

He made her feel delicate, feminine, and protected; feelings that she hadn't allowed herself for years, because there was no place for that softness when a woman had to run a ranch single-handed...

She blinked, seeing for the first time the parallel between herself and her mother—only Claire had managed the ranch and raised three young daughters at the same time, which made her life a hundred times more challenging than Tessa's.

The thought was scary and sad at the same time, as Tessa saw her future unfolding through the years ahead. Would she end up as hard and emotionless as Claire, with nothing on earth more important to her than this ranch?

Josh touched her shoulder, sending a shiver through her that had nothing to do with the dark, cool shadows in the barn. "Are you all right?"

"Fine. Totally fine." She reined in her foolish thoughts and straightened her spine. "I got your message about the pack horses. I really owe you—I would've been home after dark, and I wouldn't have caught the problem until tomorrow."

"You'll have a better alarm system after this. Your sister is bringing over her dog."

Tessa smiled at that. "No one will get past Hobo. That's one very hyper dog."

"She also called Michael, so he's aware of what happened. Did she tell you that someone must have come here a number of times to leave those toxic weeds for your horses?"

Tessa nodded, her smile fading. "I can't believe I didn't see it happening. But I'm gone so much during the day, and often get back after dark."

And it's far harder to run this place alone then I'd ever imagined.

"Someone was pretty crafty. If I hadn't been riding past on the four-wheeler, I wouldn't have noticed what those mules were eating down at the end of the pasture. You couldn't have seen it from the gate up by the barn."

"That's one of the frightening aspects of this whole situation. Someone is carefully thinking all of this through, and finding ways to cause trouble. And I don't even know why."

He glanced around, then moved to the side of the aisle and sat on a bale, propping his crutch against the stall behind him. He patted the space next to him. "Here, come into my office. We need to talk."

She wavered.

"I'm not going to bite, I promise."

That felt like a challenge, and a challenge had always been hard for her to ignore. She sat at the far end of the bale, drew her feet up, and wrapped her arms around her knees. "I need to talk to you, too."

He tipped his head in agreement, without so much as a hint of guilt or hesitation. "You first."

"Why are you here, Josh?"

He did a double take at that, then grinned. "You. Remember? You brought me here."

She waved away his words with an impatient

flip of her hand. "No. Why are you *here*—in this part of Wyoming?"

"A photo assignment, just as I said." He lifted a shoulder in a slight shrug. "Though I'm way behind on it now."

She had a feeling they'd be going in circles for the next hour, if she didn't cut to the chase. "Kirby Fellows says you've been asking a lot of questions around town. He thinks you're here to stir up trouble."

Josh angled a look at her. "Trouble?"

She reined in her impatience. "I think you know what I mean. All the photos. Talking to people. You've even done it to me—asking lots of questions about the drought, and about government grazing allotments. So is that what your trip is really about? Some sort of exposé for an environmental group?"

"I'm not here to cause you any trouble," he said after a long pause. "I'm just completing my last assignment for a magazine. But yes, I'm photographing the impact of this long-term drought."

"With a slant, right? To show that the ranchers are careless? That we're thoughtlessly overusing the land?"

"You can't deny that the land here is fragile. That the topsoil is thin and the growing season is short."

"Of course not."

"And there's already an ample elk and deer population up on those summer ranges."

"True, but *you* can't deny that the ranchers are careful. We're allowed a limited number of cattle up there, and we all follow that to the letter. And we carefully rotate those herds." She pushed off the bale and strode a few yards, then turned back, her tension rising. "That grass is lush this time of year, but it certainly isn't in our best interest to overgraze it. Why would we risk permanent damage? It would be a classic case of shooting ourselves in the foot."

"Maybe some of the other ranchers aren't quite that careful."

"So I suppose they're the ones you want to find?"

"Actually, I'm trying to present a balanced view," he said quietly.

"Right. But you didn't say a word to me until now, which implies you wanted to keep it a secret. I can just imagine how *balanced* it will be. Most of the families around here have held on to their allotments for fifty, sixty years. Without the use of that land, few of us could run enough cattle to stay in business." She clenched her fists at her side, angry at him. Disappointed at herself for not seeing his real motivation for being here.

And all too aware that once again, Claire had been right.

"Even if we're on different sides of this issue, I care about you, Tessa." He met her gaze with frank honesty in his own. "Why would I do anything to hurt you?"

Why, indeed. Memories from the past slammed into her thoughts, robbing her of coherent speech. She'd trusted him implicitly long ago. But was he really at fault for what happened? Wasn't she, as well?

He leaned back against the stall, still watching her

expression. "I'm not sure what else I can say, other than to give you my word and ask that you trust me."

She managed a faint nod.

"Not exactly an enthusiastic response, but it's a start." His mouth lifted in a faint smile as he solemnly offered his hand. "Friends—a little?"

She hesitated. "A little."

She briefly pressed his hand, all too aware of the tingling sensation that danced across her skin at his touch. Wishing she didn't still feel that same attraction.

"Good, because we need to discuss something else." The playful note in his voice vanished. "You need to think about who would profit most if this ranch or your outfitting business failed. Who would have the motivation to make that happen?"

She poked at a frayed hole in the knee of her jeans. "The other outfitters, I suppose. But most have smaller operations like mine, and I've never noticed any resentment or jealousy. The big companies shouldn't care. They've got huge budgets for advertising and have upscale facilities, and they book customers a year in advance. Why would they worry about a small operation like mine? It just doesn't make sense."

"But there's a limited pool of clients out there, and a lot of those people probably research vacation destinations all winter, looking for the best experience for their money, not necessarily a luxury package." He cocked an eyebrow. "Had any recent encounters with those other operators lately?"

"At the feed store or the grocery, now and then. We all just say hi and go on. And then there's Arlen, who owns Whiskey River Outfitters. He's always telling me that he wants to buy me out, and makes little comments about how much more successful his business is. But if he really had an agenda, I doubt he'd be so open about it."

"You don't think he's serious?"

"Oh, he's serious all right. He's got the money, and I really do think he'd like to buy me out. But I'd have to be starving to ever let that happen, because he's one of the most arrogant men I know. And honestly, my company poses little threat to his. So why would he risk legal problems by doing anything underhanded?"

"Anyone else?"

She thought for a minute. "As far as the ranch is concerned, hungry real estate investors are always looking for prime property. No one comes to mind, though."

They fell silent, listening to the sound of horses swishing their tails at flies and stamping their feet.

"The irony is that no one would have to risk doing anything aggressive," she continued. "With the drought and poor cattle prices, plus the loans we've had to take out, the financial status of this ranch is rocky. We could spiral into bankruptcy and foreclosure in the next couple years, easily."

"It can't be as bad as all that."

"No? I've got a $12,000 note due in less than two weeks. And unless I can pull together a shipment of cattle before then, I won't be able to pay it off." She felt a melancholy tug at her heart. "That would damage our credit rating, which would make future loans at a decent rate nearly impossible…and the collateral was a section of the ranch, so there we'd be in trouble, too."

"Can you pay it off?"

"You bet I will. I'll have to let some good breeding stock go, and tonight I'm listing my custom-made saddle on one of the Internet auction sites. You can't find new ones by this maker anymore, and the vintage models usually go for at least three grand."

Josh whistled under his breath. "Amazing."

"It was a gift from my Uncle Gray for my high school graduation. With the sterling conchos and lacing on the cantle and gullet, it should go for a lot more." She looked up at Josh and tried for a nonchalant tone. "There's no room for sentiment anymore. What matters is holding onto this ranch."

He hesitated, then curved an arm around her shoulders for a hug. "By this time next year, everything will be back on track. Your troublemaker will be cooling his heels in jail, the drought will be over, and cattle prices will go through the roof."

She smiled. "I like your version of the future a lot better than mine."

"Just keep an eye out, Tess. If someone is after some sort of crazy, secret retaliation against you, it can't stay a secret forever. You or someone else will notice something unusual—some clue—and we'll get it figured out before I leave here. I don't want to go until that happens."

Leave? The word startled her, and she looked up at him in surprise. She'd been hesitant about offering him a place to stay. But he'd been here over three weeks now, and he was becoming part of the fabric of life at the ranch. The thought of him moving on filled her with a sense of loss she hadn't expected.

"So…how soon will you get that cast off?" Embarrassed by the shaky note in her voice, she playfully nudged him with her elbow and slid over to the far end of the bale. "I can only imagine how much you're going to miss it."

"I'll have it at least three more weeks."

"And what about your Harley? Have you heard anything about the repairs?"

"Probably about that long, as well. The guys at the shop said they had to order a number of parts online, and that's taking longer than they expected. The bodywork is nearly completed."

So he would be gone that soon. *But it's for the best,* she reminded herself silently.

With his life established out East, he probably wouldn't be back anytime soon, while this was her home, her career, and her commitment. There was no way that she'd ever be able to leave. When he left, he would be walking out of her life for good.

He looked down at her, his eyes soft and questioning, and she had a sudden, surprising sense that he wanted to kiss her. Would he? Did she dare let him?

Her cell phone rang, jarring and insistent, saving her from a potential mistake.

But her relief was short-lived.

At the end of the terse message, she dropped the phone in her lap and stared across the aisle, filled with disbelief.

"T-that was Michael." She felt the beat of her heart mark the seconds. Slow. Steady. Yet the world had taken a dizzying spin in an unexpected direction, and she hadn't even known it until now. *Poor Danny.*

"Edward Clive was found murdered this afternoon."

"Who?"

"Danny's former stepfather—or at least, one of them. H-he owned a cabin ten miles from here." She fought down the lump in her throat, remembering the kindly old man with a shock of white hair and twinkling blue eyes who had always greeted her warmly whenever they crossed paths. "And now they've issued a warrant on Danny for the murder—but no one can find him anywhere."

THIRTEEN

With Leigh's dog Hobo now on patrol, quiet moonlight nights and the soft symphony of coyote howls in the distance were over. To Hobo, everything that moved—from June bugs to the twinkling lights of jets far overhead—were cause for alarm.

Elvis sat on the porch of the main house and watched the other Border collie in action on Wednesday night without making a sound.

He watched again on Thursday night, then apparently figured that shadowing Hobo would be a lot more fun than clinging to Josh. By ten o'clock, a duet of fierce barks erupted at the least provocation.

Maybe that racket wasn't conducive to sleeping, but Tessa had no doubt that her canine alarm system was on high alert as she worked into the early morning hours on ranch bookwork, then listed her favorite saddle on eBay.

Melancholy, she closed down the computer and wandered through the empty house, locking the doors and flipping off lights as she went.

She caught a flicker of movement at the corner of her eye as she passed the dining room. She whirled around, her heart in her throat as a dozen possibilities raced through her thoughts—and most of them weren't good.

"Who's there?" she demanded, edging backward down the hall. Without taking her eyes off the darkened opening to the dining room, she fumbled for a heavy brass vase on a small table by the open staircase.

Another ten feet and she could dart in the kitchen and race out the back door…

"It's…me."

The voice sounded as frightened as she felt herself. *"Danny?"*

He stepped out of the shadows, his clothes filthy and face ghost-white, his eyes downcast. "I-I wasn't gonna steal anything big. I just wanted to find some food. I didn't think anyone was home."

Relief flooded through her. "How on earth did you get past the dogs?"

Appearing too exhausted to stay upright for much longer, he wobbled a little and braced a hand against the wall. "They know me, I guess."

"Come on to the kitchen and I'll get you something." She looped her arm through his and took him there, settled him at the table, then foraged through the refrigerator. "This is some sort of fancy chicken fettuccini from tonight's supper," she said, showing him the bowl. "I can nuke a plate of it, if you'd like. It's really good."

He nodded, then folded his arms on the table and rested his cheek against them while Tessa microwaved an ample portion for him. She held back, not saying anything, until he'd polished off two platefuls, and a couple glasses of milk.

"You know there's a warrant out for your arrest," she said in a matter-of-fact tone.

He placed the silverware neatly on the plate and set it to one side with deliberate care, not meeting her eyes. "It's all wrong," he mumbled. "I was never anywhere close to that cabin. And I'd never hurt Edward, or anyone else."

He swiped at his eyes with the back of his wrist, and when he finally looked up at her, she could see that he'd been crying. "Where have you been?"

"H-hiding."

"I gathered that," she said dryly. "But you *know* it'll just be a matter of time before the law catches up to you. And it'll be a lot worse for you if they have to chase you down, than if you turn yourself in."

"But I didn't *do* it. Someone said they saw me at Edward's cabin just before h-he was killed. I heard it on the radio." He sucked in a shuddering breath. "But I can't prove anything, because I was alone."

"You called me Tuesday evening and said you were sick, Danny, so you couldn't come to work. That's just about the time Edward was killed."

His gaze dropped to the table top. "I *was* sick… sorta."

"Were you out drinking with your friends?"

"No!" He shook his head vehemently. "I only did that one time last winter—and I know it was just plain stupid."

"You weren't with anyone at all?"

Looking miserable, he shook his head. "Nope."

There'd been just a slight hesitation, and she wondered if maybe he'd been with a girlfriend, but it wasn't really her place to ask. She sat back in her chair and sighed. Danny was twenty-three, but right now he looked scared and defeated and much, much younger.

"The thing is, there's a warrant for your arrest, and it isn't going away. You can't run forever."

He didn't look up.

"You already know Michael, and you know he's a fair man. I'm sure the state has sent investigators to the crime scene, and they're gathering every last bit of evidence. Won't that clear your name?"

"What if it doesn't? What if they listen to those lies instead, and I end up in *prison?*"

She pushed a plate of Sofia's ginger cookies toward him and silently waited for him to sort out his thoughts.

"You might as well call," he said finally, his voice heavy. "I guess I just want to get this over."

A deputy arrived at the ranch an hour later. Tactful and businesslike, he still insisted on handcuffs and putting Danny in the back seat of the cruiser, though Danny seemed more like a frightened rabbit than some cold-blooded killer.

Which of course he wasn't. But what about his friends?

His mother had gone through too many marriages and live-in boyfriends to count. Edward had surely been a high point through all of that, but as far as Tessa knew, there'd never been a strong and consistent father figure in the picture…and that had left the boy vulnerable to the wrong crowd.

Long after she tried to fall asleep, the thought kept running through Tessa's mind. Could he be trying to protect his friends—or someone else?

The last time Tessa stepped inside the Jackson County Sheriff's Office, she'd been there to pick up one of her ranch hands after he'd gotten in a fight over some girl.

The faded green paint and scarred furniture hadn't changed, but now there was a pretty young girl at the desk instead of a stern woman with her hair wrenched into a tight bun, and several large prints of the Tetons and the Snake River hung on the cement block walls.

"Nice," Tessa ventured while she waited for Michael to come out of his office. "It's a little more cheerful in here."

The girl—Kaleesa, according to the name pin on her sweater—rolled her eyes. "The sheriff's wife wants to do a makeover in here. I'm all for it."

"How much longer will he be, do you think?"

She glanced down at the buttons on her phone. "Soon. He just ended his call."

"Can I visit Danny Watkins while I wait?"

The girl studied her cuticles. "Gotta talk to the sheriff first, in case the prisoner is dangerous."

Tessa laughed. "And do you think he is?"

"Danny? Of course not. He was in my classes all the way through school. He wouldn't hurt a flea." Her eyes rounded at her careless statement and a blush worked into her cheeks. "Um…I shouldn't have said that. Don't tell the sheriff, okay?"

Tessa nodded. A moment later, Michael's office door opened. He stepped into the hall and motioned to her, and she followed him into his office.

"So, what's his bail?" she asked as soon as Michael sat at his desk.

He fiddled with a pencil. "I'm afraid there isn't any."

"You're kidding, right?" She took the chair in front of his desk and waited for Michael to smile, but he only shook his head. "He's just a kid. You and I both know he couldn't have killed Edward, and he has a steady job at the ranch. He isn't going anywhere."

"At the arraignment this morning, the judge ruled against bail. Danny has a prior conviction—"

"For that single, wild party?"

"He was over twenty-one, he was charged, and he pleaded guilty, Tess. It's now on his record."

"That's crazy!"

"He just got probation for two years, though. With good behavior his record would have been expunged. But he also tried to avoid arrest on these current charges, so the judge deemed him a flight risk. Until the trial, Danny will be staying behind bars."

"What about a lawyer? Does he even have one?"

"A public defender. The arraignment was done by video conference this morning, but she'll be here this afternoon to meet with him."

Tessa sank into her chair, suddenly feeling faint. "And the charges?"

"Not good. Evidence found at the scene clearly placed Danny in that cabin, and his prints were on the murder weapon. Some stolen items were found in Danny's car."

"No." She closed her eyes tight for a moment, already knowing what this would mean.

Michael nodded. "Wyoming law. Murder in the first degree includes premeditated and felony murder, and the D.A. is going for the latter. Which means—"

"Don't say it. Danny would *never* have done this, Michael. I know him too well."

But Michael's unspoken words still hung in the air between them, powerful and frightening and final. For a conviction could mean the end of a young man's dreams…and his life.

Watching Tessa deal with one blow after another filled Josh with frustration and sadness. Gone was the fun-loving girl he'd dated in college—the one who had been up for every adventure, and who had marked his heart forever with her beautiful smile and absolute determination to achieve every goal she set.

Now, she looked exhausted. Frazzled. And deeply heartbroken by the turn of events with Danny, who had been in jail for almost a week now. It was as if someone had decided to take away every avenue of help for her, leaving her with overwhelming responsibilities that no single person could handle.

When she wasn't doing chores or the endless tasks involved in running a large ranch, she was dealing with the customers for her outfitting business, and without Danny to help out, she'd had to take a number of trips with clients during the last week.

All told, it was the reason he sat on an exam table at the doctor's office in Wolf Creek, and was staring down an equally determined, silver-haired physician's assistant.

"This would be against sound medical practice," she said, her arms folded across her chest. "It's only been four weeks."

"I'll be careful. I'm not planning on any marathons, and I'll keep my leg wrapped. How about that?"

"With someone your age, and with that kind of fracture, we'd *maybe* consider a walking cast about now. We certainly wouldn't just take your cast off and set you free."

"I'll sign a waiver. A release form. Anything you say, just take this thing off."

"I know it isn't pleasant," she said with a patient smile. "Everyone gets just a little stir crazy after a while."

"I'm not stir crazy. I'm *incapacitated*."

"Exactly! That's what happens when you break something," she enunciated her words a little too carefully, as if trying to get through to someone with an IQ of fifty. "And if you don't let it heal properly, you could be incapacitated for a whole lot longer. In fact, you could fracture it all over again, and then where would you be?"

He drew in a slow, steady breath, trying to hang on to his fading patience. "I need to be able to get on a horse and stay there. My cast makes that impossible. If you won't take it off, I'll need to go back to the ranch and try get it off myself…with tin snips, or a saw, or a mallet. Either way, I'll risk needing sutures, but I don't have time for that, either. I'm guessing that your refusal of care could be considered problematic if I end up with permanent injuries while trying to do your job."

She drew herself up and glared at him. "I'll have to call the doctor."

"Please do. I'd be glad to talk to him myself."

"You'll have to sign a release form."

"Not a problem."

Her shoulders sagged in defeat. "Can I at least give you a removable walking brace? It would have a rocker bottom to help you walk, so you'd be safer and more comfortable."

He suppressed the impulse to give her a hug. "Perfect!"

"We don't often do this, though. We found that people quit using the brace way too early." She regarded him with doubt in her eyes. "Can I just ask why this is so important to you right now?"

"I have a friend who needs help, badly."

The physician's assistant lifted Josh's slender file folder and turned to the face sheet. Her eyes widened as she scanned down the page. "This says you're staying at Snow Canyon Ranch."

"Just until my Harley and I are ready for the open road."

The woman's frosty demeanor melted. "Tessa needs a good friend now, though I don't suppose she'd ever admit it. With Danny in jail and Gus in rehab, I can't imagine how she's holding things together."

"That's why I'm here, ma'am," he said with a smile. He tapped the hard surface of his cast. "And the sooner you get this thing off me, the easier her life will be."

When he got back to the ranch at ten, Tessa was busy saddling a horse. She barely acknowledged his approach.

"Where are you headed?"

"I'm way late on moving one of the herd up to summer pasture, and I can't wait any longer. Once I get that done, I need to start rounding up stock for the auction at the sale barn on Wednesday night."

"Because of the loan coming due?"

She bit her lower lip as she tightened the girth. "I hope so. I also need to ship my saddle."

"The one you listed on eBay?"

She nodded. "It went for $3,600, and I need every penny of that. I'm…grateful for all the bidders."

She sounded a lot more sad than happy, though.

"If someone was going to need an experienced horse to work cattle, which one would he pick?"

"Probably Jasper, the big buckskin in the corral next to the barn." She unhooked the stirrup from the saddle horn and let it drop it into place, then unsnapped the cross-tie ropes from her gelding's halter, slipped it off, and bridled him. "Jasper's a real good cow horse, and he's dependable. Why?"

She looked over at Josh, and her gaze traveled down to his injured leg—which was now encased only in denim jeans. "What on earth did you do? It's been only what—four weeks or so?"

"I've got a removable brace in the truck, but figured it wouldn't work for riding. You need some extra help, and I'm coming along."

She shook her head firmly. "Bad idea. This'll be a long, hard day, even for me. That leg of yours has to be tender, and I can't slow down or quit to bring you back here when it starts to hurt."

He grinned. "The horse will be doing the moving, not me."

"So you think. Do you have any idea how exhausting this can be? It's not like sitting on a couch. We'll be riding on rough ground. Moving fast. The cattle don't exactly fall into a nice, easy line, so your horse might suddenly slam on the brakes, pivot, and want to chase after a straggler. You think you're ready for that?"

"Absolutely," he lied. Just walking from the truck

to the barn had made his tender leg ache and had
shown him just how weak those muscles were.

But he had a roll of Ace bandaging in his pocket,
courtesy of the medical clinic in town, and that ought
to offer plenty of support. If it didn't work well
enough, so be it.

Tessa did need help whether she wanted to admit
it or not. And even if it killed him, he wasn't going
to let her down.

"They're gone now. Let's *go*."

The smaller man sank back into the shadows. "You
don't hear that dog? It's barking its fool head off!"

"And who's gonna hear it? The kid's in jail. The
old guy is laid up in town, and that's where his wife
goes everyday. There ain't anyone here."

Still, they waited. Five minutes. Ten. From this
vantage point above the house and barns, one could
see a cloud of dust boiling up behind any vehicle traveling the mile-long ranch road leading out to the
highway, and the air was crystal clear. Off to the
right, Josh and Tessa had become small specks on the
landscape and had long disappeared into the foothills.

"You got the list? I don't want to mess this up."

"Got it. Now, let's *go*."

The dogs had made it too risky last night. With all
that barking, it had been better to retreat than to risk
the business end of Tessa McAllister's rifle.

But daylight had its own risks, even with everyone
at the ranch gone. They'd had to come across country

on foot to avoid being seen. It would be a long hike back with what they took.

But it was worth it…every last step. Debts needed to be paid, after all.

And this would be the perfect repayment of one that was long overdue.

FOURTEEN

Riding Jasper out to the pasture with Tessa and her horse Dusty was an easy trip. They crossed gently rolling land, passing through a series of gates between the various pastures, with the warm June sun high overhead and a growing, easy camaraderie that had them laughing most of the way.

The tricky part was when they actually *reached* the cattle in question. Tessa promptly disappeared over the next hill, heading toward the western reaches of the pasture at a lope.

She'd shouted directions as she rode off—nothing that Josh had heard clearly over the thunder of Dusty's hooves and the bawling cattle, but the goal seemed clear enough: gather all of the cows and drive them north.

Only it wasn't obvious to the cows.

They were scattered over hundreds of acres, standing in shady draws to escape the flies, spread out on the hillsides, or having little one-on-one chats deep within nearly impenetrable thickets.

As soon as he had a few of them heading in the right direction, a couple of them would veer away. If he got a few dozen cornered and went off to gather some more, the original group declared recess and trotted off.

It had to approximate trying to herd cats or goldfish, and both the tenderness in his leg and his impatience were growing. Where were the obedient, well-trained herds of the old John Wayne movies, that moved en masse like dark, thick molasses?

Even Jasper seemed irritated by the whole process.

He tossed his head and danced sideways, obviously disagreeing with Josh's supervision. He could only imagine that Tessa, alone with her horse, was facing the same problem.

That misconception was promptly dispelled when he heard the rumble of hooves approaching, and looked up to see a solid flood of beef pouring over the hill with Tessa and her horse neatly maneuvering the herd from behind.

"Open the gate!" she shouted, cupping one hand at her mouth.

The gate? He pivoted Jasper toward the north and, following the direction she pointed out, kicked him into fourth gear, and reached it with seconds to spare. As soon as the cattle went through, he pushed the heavy pipe gate shut.

Tessa pulled to halt next to him. "There's fifty," she said, pushing up the brim of her hat and wiping away the sweat on her brow. "How about you?"

"Mine are...taking a break."

"You've got *none?*"

"I had quite a few, now and then, but I didn't know you wanted me to drive them into that other pasture, and the cows lost interest in standing around. They can't be too far, though."

"That other 'pasture' is a two-acre holding pen. Since they've had a little practice heading this way, we shouldn't have any trouble if you'll just watch the gate. Shall we?"

She gave her horse an almost imperceptible signal, and it did a hundred-eighty degree pivot, then took off at a lope, swinging wide around a half-dozen cows and calves.

She and Dusty made it look effortless as the horse ducked his head low and darted back and forth as gracefully as a ballet dancer, blocking escape attempts and working cows and calves into a tight bunch, then sending them on through the gate.

In another hour, Tessa had rounded up the rest of the cattle, counted them off, and the herd was on its way down a narrow gravel lane that wound up into the foothills, until it reached the government allotment where they would summer on better grass.

Once the herd was through that final gate, Tessa padlocked it, then rested an elbow on her saddle horn and propped her chin on her palm. He thought she was just resting, until he realized that she was counting the slowly dispersing herd one last time.

"They sure are far from home up here. Is theft a big problem?"

"It happens. My ten head of missing mother cows haven't turned up yet. Eight were our own breeding stock, which we've been carefully developing for decades, but two came from a herd genetically engineered for top production results, and I hate to add up what we lost."

"Ballpark?"

She winced. "I had around $4,000 in each of the two new ones, and the others were easily two grand apiece at auction. If they're sitting in someone's freezer, it's a tremendous waste of breeding potential."

He looked out over the cattle they'd just brought up here. "So, what's to prevent someone from taking these?"

"The more often I can get up here to count 'em, the better. If anything takes a walk—unplanned—I call the sheriff right away, and then send notices to him and all of the sales barns. The auction houses watch out for them, but sometimes it's one of the bidders who happens to see a flyer on the wall and calls in a report. Anything that works, right?"

For so much of the time since he'd come here, Tessa had been busy from dawn to dark, and he'd barely seen her, much less spoken to her for any length of time.

Now, they slipped into casual conversation about the weather, the auction coming up next week and her plans for expanding her breeding program for high-yield Angus cattle, and it took him back to the days when they'd sat in his old Chevy Malibu, talking for hours.

He studied her animated gestures and shining eyes as she discussed ranch business, realizing for the first time just how much knowledge and expertise she had to possess to make this place float.

"So, any news about Gus?"

"After rehab, he and Sofia can stay as long as they like at the ranch. I think they want to move to Colorado, though, because they have a daughter in Denver." She smiled sadly. "It just won't be the same if those two leave. They're like my family."

"What about Danny?"

"Still in jail, and that's such a waste. He should be out here, working and doing what he loves best." Her eyes sparked with anger. "If he wasn't set up, I'll eat my boots."

"There were fingerprints, though. And there were stolen goods in Danny's truck," Josh said gently. "Word has it that the state has a strong case against him."

She twisted in her saddle to look over at him. "But think about it. *Really.* Edward was Danny's stepfather for a few years, so Danny may well have been in that cabin a number of times as a visitor. So there you go—fingerprints. He probably handled Edward's gun collection many times. He might've even visited Edward that day—and the real killer saw that, and figured out the perfect way to shift the blame."

"But the stolen goods?"

"*Were* they stolen? Danny says no—that they were a gift. And I believe him."

She seemed so absolutely loyal to her young friend, despite the evidence against him, that Josh smiled.

"Do you ever wonder what would've happened if we hadn't had that last fight, back in college?" he said. "How life would have been different if we hadn't lost touch?"

"*Lost touch?*" She shot an unreadable look at him. "Do you mean—if you hadn't just dropped off the face of the planet and disappeared?" She turned away to stare at the horizon. "Yes—I suppose I thought about it a time or two."

Her words were light, but even after all these years, her voice vibrated with a depth of emotion that surprised him. "I was devastated when we broke up," he said quietly.

She laughed. "Oh, I can imagine how much. I tried to find you, but you were gone…and you sure never came back." She slid a cold glance at him. "It didn't take long to realize that I'd just been another foolish little girl with stars in her eyes, and had read *way* too much into that relationship."

"What?" He blinked, trying to sort out a version of the past that was different from everything he remembered.

"But as one of our presidents said, 'mistakes were made' and both of us moved on."

"You said you never wanted to see me again, and you made that *crystal* clear. I did try calling a couple

times, but your roommates said you refused to come
to the phone. Then my father died and I had to move
back East, because my mom just fell apart. I had
younger brother and sisters to worry about, so I trans-
ferred to a college out there."

"And I tried to find you, too. But my letters were
returned, and back then we couldn't search for old
friends using the Internet." The anger in her eyes faded
to infinite sadness. "Then I guess that's just how it was
meant to be. Two people at cross purposes...ending
up on different paths. Things always end up for the
best, right?"

Maybe she thought so, but he'd had an aching,
empty place in his heart for years afterward. He'd
relived their last argument a thousand times, trying
to figure out how things could have been so perfect
between them—yet suddenly crash and burn in a
single, devastating evening, over a minor disagree-
ment about the future that had escalated out of control. She'd hinted at wanting commitment. He'd been
startled into some sort of off-hand dismissal that had
set her off.

"I barely remember what we argued about, Tessa,
but I'm sorry." He grinned at her. "I'm sure I was
totally wrong."

"I'm sure you were," she retorted, a faint, sad
smile touching her lips. "But I had a lot on my mind
right then, and I was in a touchy mood. It doesn't
matter now, anyway. Race you to that boulder?"

Without waiting for a reply, she nudged her horse

and took off, her long, shimmering hair flying behind her as her horse thundered down the path.

Jasper danced in place, impatient to follow, until Josh gave him his head and let him fly.

By late evening, Josh knew two things: that he'd be willing to empty his bank account for a good, hot shower, and that he couldn't wait to put on his removable leg brace.

Tessa had been right.

Twelve hours of herding cattle over rough country was nothing like a leisurely ride in Central Park. Maneuvering cattle through boulder-strewn pastures and keeping them together across lush, inviting meadows involved speed, agility and endurance, and he was pretty sure that every single muscle he owned was strained to the limit.

But he would've done it all over in a heartbeat.

No matter what she said, he couldn't imagine Tessa being able to handle all those cattle without any help. And now, her cattle were on the summer range, and two dozen market-ready steers were in one of the pastures close to the barns, ready to be hauled to auction.

At the barn, Tessa dismounted lightly. Josh eyed the ground with some trepidation, then eased carefully out of the saddle to avoid landing on his injured leg.

"I'll take care of him for you," she called out as she lugged her tack into the barn.

He unsaddled Jasper on his own, dropped the saddle on the hitching rail, and led the horse into the corral. As soon as he was free, Jasper circled with his nose to the ground, then rolled vigorously, sending clouds of dust into the air.

Josh knew exactly how he felt. Smiling, he turned, then stopped.

Tessa stood in the doorway of the barn, her face pale, and her cell phone at her ear. And given her agitated gestures, something was terribly wrong.

It wasn't just the sense of violation at finding her tack room in disarray, with bridle leather slashed and saddles damaged and the phone jerked from the wall. It was the sheer waste of it all. Beautiful equipment, destroyed.

And then there was her beloved saddle. It had been a gift from Uncle Gray that she'd lovingly preserved, and rarely used. It was the one she'd sacrificed for the ranch, by selling it online, and it was to be shipped tomorrow.

Only it was gone—stolen by the vandals who had ruined almost every other piece of equipment in the tack room.

Michael had arrived several hours later to take her statement and write up a report, though that had seemed like yet another exercise in futility. There were far bigger cases to pursue in the county. Arson and burglary and domestic abuse, and she could hardly expect him to be at her constant beck and call.

What was that report, but just another document that would just sit in a file cabinet? Nothing would change.

"I don't understand," she said bitterly as she and Josh arrived back at the ranch after the cattle auction on Wednesday night. "I've done nothing underhanded to anyone. I try to be a good neighbor, and I couldn't work any harder. Yet every time I turn around, something else happens."

Josh reached across the bench seat of the pickup and squeezed her hand. "It's going to end. Sooner or later, this guy is going to slip up, and he'll be caught. It's going to take him a long time to pay restitution, while sitting behind bars. Have you heard anything more from Michael?"

"Nope. I did an Internet search of tack stores, commercial stables and sales barns in a six-state area, though, and faxed a description of my saddle to every one of them. And, I'm monitoring the online auction sites for saddle listings."

"What did your saddle buyer say?"

"He e-mailed back and said not to worry, but I still have to refund his money. And if the saddle does turn up, it would only be fair to offer it to him again." She stared out the front window at the dizzying flash of road signs illuminated by the headlights. "At least the cattle sold high enough that I can pay off that bank note tomorrow. Good news, right?"

It *was* good news. She ought to be happy. But today, a motorcycle shop in Jackson had called Josh with the news that his Harley was ready to roll... which meant he was closer to leaving.

Leigh had come out again to check on the pack

horses, and one of them had gone into liver failure. If things didn't improve by tomorrow, it would have to be euthanized rather than to let it suffer. And Danny was still refusing to talk about where he'd been on the day of Edward's murder.

So really, what else could possibly go wrong?

FIFTEEN

Tessa glanced at her watch, then stepped out of her truck and strode to the Wolf Creek Bank. Five minutes to spare, before her appointment with the loan officer. Then she needed to hurry back to the ranch and get ready for an overnight pack trip with six customers from New Jersey.

It was an unexpected booking and a welcome, big-ticket sale, and she couldn't afford to say no.

After spending a half-hour on the phone yesterday, she tracked down one of the girls who'd worked for her last summer. Kelsey Sanders, a ranch girl with common sense and a lifetime of experience in the area, had just arrived home from her junior year in college, and was more than happy to come back for a summer job.

Hiring her again was a true blessing, because it was proving nearly impossible to lead trail rides and pack trips, while keeping up with the chores at the ranch. And though Janna hadn't said anything, it had been over two weeks since Tessa had been able to pick up Claire for a day, to give Janna a breather.

This afternoon, once Kelsey and the clients were on their way, Tessa could catch up on that responsibility, too.

"Going somewhere in a hurry?"

She looked over at the row of pickups diagonally parked along the sidewalk and found Arlen Foreman standing at the door of a smoke-gray Ford, with Whiskey River Outfitters emblazoned on the side. He usually wore an arrogant, self-satisfied smile, but today he looked anything but pleased.

"Just errands."

"I was planning to call you." His eyes narrowed and he slammed the door shut, then came to stand in front of her on the sidewalk. "Don't think I'm unaware of what you did, McAllister."

A few passersby slowed and gave them both curious looks.

"I have no idea what you're talking about, Arlen. Is something wrong?"

He swore under his breath and took a step closer, so she had to tip her head up to look at him. "Friendly competition is one thing." His voice grew harsh, and louder, and now people across the street stopped to stare. "But stealing customers—good, long-term customers—is something else."

She stood her ground, rather than back away. "Again—I don't know what you're talking about. So if you'll excuse me?"

She moved to go around him, but he stepped in her way. "I had a group scheduled this week. Six people, for their annual trip. Then I get a call yesterday and they cancel, saying they could get much better guides and a better rate through you."

"I did get a call—and I did book a group of six. But they contacted me, not vice versa, and it's a free country, Arlen. If they were willing to give up their deposit, then they do have a right to change. Maybe they just started cruising Web sites, or something."

"You really don't want me for an enemy, Tessa," he said, his urbane facade dissolving before her eyes. "I hadn't been too worried about your little hobby, but when you start pulling this sort of thing, you're just asking for trouble."

Trouble—as in what she'd been having during the past month?

"Tell me, Arlen," she lowered her voice and fixed her eyes on his, feeling her anger rise. "What do you know about yellow star thistle?"

"What?"

"And what about nice old custom-made saddles— got any extras?"

He took a half-step back. "I have *no* idea what you mean. But believe me, I'm not done talking to you about those customers. You can expect to hear from my lawyer by tomorrow. No underhanded cheat of a—"

"*Stop.* Unless you want to hear from *my* lawyer about slander?"

The tone always worked on dogs, and it tended to work on men, too. Arlen's mouth snapped shut, and he glanced around at the growing number of people who were watching them with open curiosity.

"Your lawyer can visit with me all he wants, because I've done nothing wrong." She lowered her voice even further, for his ears only. "And *you* can expect a visit from the sheriff, because I think you've just made his job a lot easier."

This time, she did step around him. Glancing at her watch, she hurried up the steps of the bank and pulled to a halt in front of the receptionist's desk. "Ellen Miller?"

The woman looked toward an open office door, where Ellen could be seen standing at her desk with her purse in hand. "I'm not sure. I think she's just leaving for lunch. Can you come back?"

"I'm sorry, but I can't…and this has to be done today."

With a wave of her fingertips, Tessa strode to the office, rapped on the door frame, and walked in.

Ellen's automatic smile faltered when Tessa took a chair and sat down. "I'm leaving, Ms. McAllister. You're *late*. And I really don't have any time to discuss loans extensions with you. I think you already have the bank's answer?"

"And this is mine—payment in full, and on time." She rose halfway and handed an envelope across the desk. "It's a cashier's check for $14,768.00, from the Salt Creek Sales Barn. I'd like the rest deposited in my savings account."

"W-what on earth did you sell?" The other woman

fumbled for the backrest of her desk chair and sat down before opening the envelope.

"Cattle—including a couple of top cows that we were going to use as embryo transfer donors. They went for around $5,000 apiece."

Ellen blinked. "Well. This is certainly a surprise."

She reached for her phone and punched a button, then talked quietly to someone, twisting a strand of her curly auburn hair around her index finger as she spoke.

Tessa settled back in her chair, feeling a rush of relief. One problem down, a hundred to go—but with every small victory, the future of the ranch was more secure…

She idly glanced at the framed college degrees and awards certificates on the walls, and on a bookshelf by the door, the usual display of family photos that seemed to be standard issue in every office. The kids. The dog. Rows of relatives lined up in front of a fireplace, looking stiff and awkward, ready to flinch when the camera flashed.

In a photo of children playing, she recognized the old Wolf Creek Elementary School in the background. In another, the same kids were on the swings at the town square…

The receiver of Ellen's phone dropped noisily in its cradle. "Toni has the loan documents in her files," Ellen said. "I'm sure you'd like to get this done quickly and be on your way, and I need to leave. Come with me."

Ellen ushered her to the other office and made

the introduction, then handed Toni the cashier's check and left.

The young woman smiled and waved Tessa to a seat next to her desk. "Do you have your checking account number?"

"I—oops, I left my purse in the other office. I'll be right back." Tessa turned on her heel and went next door to Ellen's office, grabbed her purse from the floor and turned to go...

She blinked as she passed the bookshelf, then looked back.

The photos of those children were missing.

At the sound of tires crunching on gravel, Josh saved the file he was working on and closed the lid of his laptop.

He was nearly done with his article for the magazine, and now he had only to sort through the hundreds of digital photos he'd been taking. With the deadline just two days away, it would be a relief to get it all finished and e-mailed...and then, maybe, he could try to finagle Tessa into finding some time away from the ranch, just the two of them.

Here, there were constant interruptions and end-less chores, and the stress had to be overwhelming. But away—even if just into town for a quiet dinner— maybe they could sit down and really talk, finally. To settle the past, once and for all, and maybe even set the groundwork for building a deeper relationship.

Was there any chance, with her?

With each passing day, he found himself drawn to her all the more. There couldn't be another woman on the planet as unique as her—so pretty, but without artifice. Intelligent, and driven, and insightful—yet with a tender, sentimental side that she carefully tried to hide.

He'd seen it in her deep regret over her beloved saddle. Her worries about her mother's old horse, and the welfare of those pack horses. If someone helped shoulder her burdens and brought love into her life, would she be a happier person?

Maybe there wasn't even a chance of becoming a part of her life. He still sensed her wall of reserve and had noticed her veiled expression at times when he caught her looking at him.

She was probably just counting the days until he could climb on his Harley and head East.

The sound of women's voices drifted in through his open windows. Sofia and Claire, he realized as he hobbled to the door of his cabin and stepped outside to say hello.

Janna was behind the wheel of her truck visiting with them, but drove off a moment later, leaving Claire behind.

Sofia looked toward him and waved. "I'll be here all day," she called out. "Be sure to come over for lunch at noon. And supper, too—I'll be making enchiladas."

"Thanks!" He went back to his laptop to finish the article, but found himself looking out the window, lost in thought.

Since her husband's heart attack, Sofia had been welcoming and friendly, though Claire had become increasingly distant—even surly—whenever she saw Josh.

He understood Alzheimer's and how it could create such hardships for family members trying to keep their loved ones home. He knew that she must have been a fine woman in her day, and he could handle her narrow-eyed stares and her silence toward him.

But the sharp, critical way she spoke to Tessa set his teeth on edge. He wanted to defend Tessa. Shelter her from her mother's behavior. Yet what could he do? It was the older woman's mental deterioration talking, not the woman she was inside.

At the sound of footsteps on the porch he looked up. And there was Claire herself, glaring at him through the screen door, as if she'd heard his thoughts and was zeroing in on her newest prey.

Where was Sofia?

He set his laptop aside once more and rose. "Um…hello, Claire. Would you like me to walk you back to the house?"

She silently jerked the door open and came inside, an eerie expression glittering in her eyes. "You think I don't remember."

He tried for a friendly smile. "Remember?"

"But I do remember—all of us do." Her voice was flat, oddly monotone, as if she were reciting something from a script. "You're not welcome here, and you need to *leave*."

He kept his smile in place. "I do plan to leave soon, Claire."

"It's not soon enough!" Her voice rose, and she started across the floor toward him, her face contorted with sudden rage. "You thought you could come here, and ruin things again? Hurt my daughter?"

He edged over to the coffee table and picked up his cell phone. Holding it at his side, he flipped it open, then he glanced down and speed dialed Tessa's house. *Please Sofia…answer the phone…*

It rang…six, seven times, then the answering machine kicked in. He left a brief message and snapped the cell phone closed, without taking his eyes off Claire. Would Sofia even check messages on Tessa's phone? Probably not.

"I'll be gone very soon," he said in a low, soothing tone, extending his hands palms up. "I'm only here by accident. I don't want to harm anyone. Tessa is a *friend*."

He eyed the room for anything she could use as a weapon, unsure of her intentions. He'd been in a lot of tight situations and could hold his own in a fight. But dealing with an elderly, fragile woman was something else entirely, and he only wanted to keep her from hurting herself.

"You don't treat *friends* like trash." Her voice turned bitter and her eyes took on a faraway look, as if she were seeing something painful from the past. "You don't use them and throw them away like garbage."

"Of course not, Claire. No good friend would ever do that. And I wouldn't think of it." He nodded toward the oak rocking chair in the corner. "Would you like to sit down? I could get you some tea or water."

From outside came the distant sound of Sofia's voice, calling Claire's name over and over.

Her attention riveted on Josh, she didn't appear to hear the housekeeper. "You preyed on my girl," she snarled. "My innocent daughter."

He relaxed a little at that. "Is that what this is about? She and I dated in college. I loved her, Claire, but we broke up."

"Loved her? You say you *loved* her?" Claire's fists clenched at her sides. "You got her pregnant, and you walked out on her, you lousy excuse for a man."

He felt the blood drain from his face. "No...I didn't."

Sofia appeared at the door, her face a mask of worry. "Claire," she whispered, reaching for the other woman's arm. "It's time to go. You're tired."

Claire twisted away and stumbled against the wall, her eyes darting between them. "*Tell* him," she ground out. "*Tell* him what he did."

Sofia lifted her pain-filled gaze to meet Josh's, and in that moment his blood turned to ice and he *knew* what she was going to say. "I...had no idea."

"Claire and Tessa both tried for months to find you. But the college couldn't give out your information, of course. And apparently you left no forwarding address, because Tessa's letters all came back."

"See! It's true—and now here you are. Did you think you could use her all over again?" Claire angrily shook off Sofia's gentle touch. "It won't happen."

"She and I had broken up. She refused to even talk to me after that. My father passed away, so I left the next day, then dropped out of school and stayed out East to help my family."

The enormity of what had happened settled on him like a suffocating blanket. What had Tessa gone through, all alone? Having to face her family. Her friends. Having to go through an unplanned pregnancy…and it didn't take much imagination to see that Claire had probably been hard and unforgiving, every step of the way.

But there was no baby here…no little girl or boy with strawberry blond hair and Tessa's boundless energy. He suddenly felt sick. "Did…did she end the pregnancy?"

Claire's rage slowly faded, leaving her gaunt face defeated and drawn, and she finally let Sofia lead her to a chair.

"Claire insisted on giving the baby up for adoption, but Tessa refused. She fought her mom for the entire nine months, because Claire was so angry that a daughter had failed her."

He waited, feeling breathless and disconnected to everything but the sound of Sofia's rich, deep voice. "And?"

The woman's eyes shimmered. "She had that

baby, a little boy. So beautiful, so perfect. She named him Joshua. But there were problems—and he only lived a few minutes. He died in Tessa's arms."

SIXTEEN

Josh stared at the walls for an hour after Sofia and Claire left, feeling more alone and empty than he'd ever felt before.

He'd been a little wild during his early college days, so far from home and away from parental supervision. He'd reveled in his freedom, and had partied too much, stayed up too late, then slept through most of each weekend, never bothering to get up for church. He'd missed too many classes and let his GPA slip. It had been all too easy to fall in with the wrong crowd.

But his relationship with Tessa had been a fragile, gentle thing, filled with wonder and the thrill of a first, young love. He'd started to clean his act up after he met her, for she was an innocent ranch girl and shied away from the wild crowd, and he'd wanted to be with her every moment of every day.

He searched his memory, trying to remember the day they broke up. So close to that one, fateful night when they'd gone further than they'd meant to…. Had she already been afraid she could be pregnant?

Had she been scared and tense and trying to tell him about it? He sure hadn't gotten the message. Had he inadvertently said something that devasted her?

For any teenager, an unplanned pregnancy would be a frightening situation. With a mother like Claire waiting back at the ranch, it must have been terrifying.

And just like he had with Lara, Josh now knew that he must have failed Tessa every step of the way.

He didn't even want to imagine the depths of grief she must have felt while holding her sweet baby in her arms and watching him die.

There were no words Josh could say, there was no way he could repair the damage he had done. No wonder Tessa had given him such a cool reception—what had it been like for her, seeing a nightmare from her past come to life? And now he'd stayed at her ranch, dragging out those terrible memories for six long weeks.

Maybe he'd had some hopes and dreams about rekindling a relationship with her—one that could last forever—but the only fair thing would be to pack up and get out of her life…and leave her in peace.

Tessa pulled to a stop in front of the barn at six o'clock. Turned off the motor of the truck, then leaned against the seat, lost in thought.

She'd mulled over the past couple months on her way back to the ranch. None of the pieces seemed to fit, yet sheer coincidence was improbable at best. How could so many things happen and not be related?

The wildfires in the area were an annual problem, of course. And though the fire season rarely started this early, none of them had been major fires, and none had reached the Snow Canyon Ranch borders. Yet.

The cabin break-ins were scattered in a five-mile radius of Wolf Creek, so those also seemed unrelated to what had happened at the ranch—though with Danny's arrest for burglary and Edward's murder, she'd lost a valuable, essential employee.

But the cattle thefts, break-ins, and the poisoning of her pack string were another matter. Though what could be the motivation?

Competition, as Josh had suggested? She only had to look as far as Arlen for that. He'd offered to buy her out a couple times, and he'd been furious this afternoon, assuming that she'd stolen his customers. Though there could be other operators who were desperately hanging on, and ready to trample their competition in any way they could.

Or was it someone who simply hoped the ranch would go under? There wasn't a month that went by without some hotshot realtor stopping by to make an offer. Snow Canyon Ranch had perfect views of the mountains, with deeply rolling foothills, mountain streams and good pastures, and she knew any one of them—or some millionaire investor—would snap up the place in a second if it ever came on the market.

And that left those who might have more personal reasons. A list of people who went way back, to when Claire had been a powerful force in the county, with powerful ties. She'd been ruthless and unforgiving, and Tessa was pretty sure that she and her sisters knew only a fraction of what had gone on.

She could only remember a couple names... though she could recall all too well the taunts of other kids at school, especially when Claire had done something particularly noteworthy.

After chores and supper, she would call Leigh and Janna, and try to come up with a list of possibilities. And then, she was going to get to work.

Sofia looked troubled when Tessa walked in the kitchen an hour later. "Janna brought Claire by this afternoon, to save you a trip," she murmured as she stirred a pot of fragrant chili on the stove.

Tessa winced. "I knew she was coming and that you'd be here, but I meant to get back much sooner. Where is she?"

"Gone."

Surprised, Tessa glanced around the kitchen. "Is she outside?"

"Janna came back and got her, because she got really agitated and it took her a while to settle down. You...probably need to visit with Josh."

Tessa groaned. "She didn't go after him. Tell me she didn't."

"Your sister says she refused to go to her last doctor's appointment but thinks maybe a medicine adjustment could help. They were headed straight for the clinic, so Claire couldn't back out again."

Tessa felt a stab of guilt. "I should've been here. Maybe I could've helped. Talked her out of it, or something."

"Your mother was beyond gentle conversation. I'm even wondering if they'll hospitalize her a while, just to get her stabilized." Sofia dropped her gaze to the chili. "I'm afraid...well, I don't know how much you've told him, but he knows everything now."

A sick feeling pooled in Tessa's stomach.

On the horrific day of her son's birth, she'd catapulted from the greatest joy on earth into the deepest chasm of grief.

After the simple graveside services, the entire family had carefully skirted the topic. Perhaps, in some misguided way, they'd figured that not mentioning her loss meant she wouldn't think about it, wouldn't mourn.

As if.

She'd mourned privately, caught in a mire of grief and guilt over the fact that she hadn't wanted the baby. Had he been somehow aware of her feelings before his birth? Felt unloved? The inestimable sadness of it all had been simply overwhelming.

In time, she'd made it vehemently clear to the family that she preferred silence to platitudes, so no one ever brought up the subject again.

Until now.

"I'm afraid your mother wasn't tactful about it," Sofia continued. "Josh looked white as snow by the time I found her."

"I...I'll talk to him. I guess I should've already, but it seemed like there wasn't a point any longer."

"There is now, honey, because I think that poor boy is upset." She waved her big wooden spoon toward the door. "And you've got an hour before suppertime to make it right."

Tessa left messages for Leigh and Janna about delving into Claire's more unfortunate business dealings with the people of Wolf Creek, then she took a deep breath, steeled herself, and hiked over to Josh's cabin.

She faltered to a stop at the sight of him standing by his vintage Harley.

"Looks like new, doesn't it?" he asked, glancing up at her. "I called the shop this afternoon and they were able to deliver it for an extra fifty bucks."

"I-it's beautiful." He went back to methodically wiping invisible dust off the chrome with one of his T-shirts, and she remembered how proud of it he'd been in college, how careful. "You don't seem pleased, though."

"I am. It runs like a dream, too. I won't have any trouble getting back to D.C."

Seeing him with that stark, sad expression in his eyes, she recognized the emotions that she'd struggled with for so long—the incredible, earth-shaking reality of being a new parent, the devastation of loss. The two farthest ends of the spectrum of human emotion, with the power to wrench your heart from your chest and grind it to dust.

She walked up to him and rested a hand on his arm, knowing that there were no words that could erase this kind of pain. Even though his loss had happened years ago, it was new to him right now.

"I'm sorry," she whispered. "I tried so hard to find you. For months and months, figuring you had the right to know. And then the baby came and…and…" She drew in a shuddering breath. "After that, I tried once last time, then gave up. I was down so low, for so long, that I didn't care about anything anymore."

He looked at her with those beautiful, sad eyes, and she automatically moved into his embrace to lay her cheek against his hard muscled chest, just as if she'd never left, never stopped loving him. It felt so *right,* feeling the steady beat of his heart and the warm strength of his arms.

He held her close, his cheek resting against her hair. "I had no idea. You've got to believe that," he murmured. "If I'd known, I would have been at your side through that whole nine months."

"I know, Josh. I know."

She'd railed at God and at Josh from the depths of her grief. For years, she'd held onto her anger, for she'd felt betrayed and abandoned by them both. After all she'd endured from Claire during the pregnancy, how could God have taken away the baby, too?

She'd mostly healed, over time. Lost that knife edge of pain in her heart. But she'd stayed away from church and had held on to the remnants of her anger for all these years. Yet now, the last of it dissipated, like faint wisps of fog in sunlight.

"I would have grieved with you. I…just had no idea. I let you down, in every possible way. And the baby…I never got to see him. My own son."

She pulled away, her hands on his forearms. "I have a baby book, with his picture and footprints, and a curl of his hair. There's…not much else in there. There wasn't time."

"Is it here—at the house?"

"Wait, and I'll get it."

She jogged back to the house and upstairs to the spare room that had once been set up as a nursery, where she'd refused to dismantle the crib and changing table for months, and where she'd hidden away to cry whenever she could.

But Claire hadn't understood. She'd somehow expected that Tessa would be back in the saddle in no time, perhaps even be relieved at the simplification of her life. And then one day, the baby clothes and furnishings simply disappeared; a violation that Tessa had never quite been able to forgive.

It had been years since Tessa had come in this room, and though Sofia kept it dusted and aired, the book was exactly where she'd left it on a nightstand, with candles and a dried, crumbling bouquet still in the original vase, with faded blue ribbon hanging limply from its neck.

When she handed the book to Josh, she saw his gentle, reverent touch of the cover, then she withdrew to the house and gave him time alone.

But after supper, they slowly walked the ranch lane clear out to the highway and back again, talking about old times. Old regrets. And by the time she wished him good night and went back to the house, she knew that she'd fallen just a little more in love with the man from her past.

Janna and Leigh both called the next morning with the names they remembered, and Tessa came up with a list of at least six families who had been harmed in some way by Claire's callous determination to profit in every way she could.

The sisters had been just little girls back then. If they remembered that many names, how many more were there?

Tessa looked through old ranch files stored in the attic, searching for employee records, then ticked down the list.

Ted Foster had worked on the ranch for fifteen years, but when Claire fired him for "insubordination"…soon after he'd been diagnosed with emphysema.

Bill Clark had sustained hip and back injuries after being bucked off a colt. He'd eventually come back to work, Tessa remembered, but then he was let go for unknown reasons.

The Haskins, though Leigh said the elder Haskins

was in desperately poor health and housebound, and his son was serving time in prison.

The Farleys, a family with a pack of small children who lived in a rental house Claire owned in town. Years ago, Claire evicted them just before the holidays for nonpayment of rent. Sure, they'd been months and months behind, but before the *holidays?* The timing had polarized the town for weeks.

And finally, there were a couple of families, the Bassetts and the Irwins, who'd had their ranching operations foreclosed. Some said that Claire had pulled strings at the local bank—after which she snapped up their property at rock-bottom prices.

Tessa turned to her laptop computer—the desktop had been at the tech shop since the break-in—and began researching each name. Using the free "people search" functions online, she looked for addresses, relatives and phone numbers, then began calling.

Ted Foster had died in Oklahoma ten years ago— too long ago and too far away to be a credible lead. Bill Clark was in a nursing home in Colorado now, with no close next of kin. The Haskins were accounted for—which left just three, and both the Irwins and the Bassetts still had Jackson County addresses. *Bingo.*

They were her only leads so far, and this afternoon, she was going into town to hunt them down.

SEVENTEEN

By the time she finished chores and working several two-year-olds in the arena, it was nearly three o'clock and she still hadn't checked on the cattle. Even if she skipped that, there wasn't much time for a shower, the drive into town, and finding people who might be able to provide the information Tessa needed.

But when Josh offered to take the four-wheeler out to check on the cattle, she gratefully accepted the help and made it through her shower and the trip to Wolf Creek in record time.

It was only when she arrived that she realized how awkward her questions were going to be. *Hey, I'm trying to find my mom's old enemies, because one of them might be trying to destroy us. Got any idea where these people are?*

Taking a fortifying breath, she stepped into the tiny Wolf Creek Post Office, where silver-haired Mrs. Halloway was selling a book of stamps to a customer. She'd been behind that counter since Tessa could remember.

The customer lingered, chatting about someone named Madge who needed surgery, and the Johnson boy who was seeing the Ralston's oldest daughter, and a host of other bits of gossip, until Mrs. Halloway held up her hand and looked over the woman's shoulder at Tessa. "Can I help you with something?"

The customer clearly wasn't leaving. The last thing Tessa needed was to ask questions in front of her, and then alert the entire gossip grapevine in town. And if Mrs. Halloway was happily exchanging news with this woman, maybe she wouldn't be such a safe bet, either.

"Um...no. I'll come back another time." She slipped out the front door and scanned the two-block long downtown area.

There were so many new shops now and many of the old standbys had closed. To the right she could just see the snow-white spire of the Wolf Creek Community Church, where her family had gone for generations.

It had been a long, long time since she'd stepped inside those massive oak doors. She found herself walking down the street in that direction, and in no time she was there, looking up the long concrete walk, she hesitated, feeling a little awkward and unsure.

And maybe a little embarrassed, given her years of absence. Her sudden appearance was for selfish reasons that had nothing to do with faith and the deepest feelings in her heart.

It was a lovely, old-fashioned church, sitting on the hillside with its tall, snowy white spire trimmed with fanciful gingerbread, and a dozen tall, stained glass windows on each side. The mullioned windows in the heavy oak doors at the front caught the sunlight and sparkled with hints of rich jewel colors, even from the distance.

There wouldn't be anyone there, though. It had been silly to come this far for nothing.

But as she turned to go, the faint strains of an organist playing "Beautiful Savior" filtered out to the street, and she noticed that those front doors were ajar. Curious, Tessa paused to listen. Was Mrs. Sawyer still the organist?

She couldn't be. Not after all these years. Her soft, white curls had bounced along in time to the hymns she played back when Tessa and her sisters were kids. If the woman had looked ancient then, she surely couldn't be alive and playing the organ now.

Still, Tessa found herself walking up that sidewalk and easing that door open a little wider, then she stepped into the cool, dark depths of the church to the familiar scents of old hymnals and cut flowers and burnished wood, which…oddly…made her feel as if she'd just come home.

The music stopped. Up at the front, to the left of the pulpit in the organist's alcove, a white head popped up from behind the organ and Mrs. Sawyer peered out over the empty pews, as spry as ever.

Tessa had always shied away from public displays

of emotion. Special notice always made her uncomfortable. She steeled herself, already embarrassed over what the elderly woman would say. *Well, well! Amazing that you walked in this door!* Or *good heavens, why on earth did you decide to come here after all these years?*

If Tessa had ever had a thought of coming back into the fold, running the gauntlet of stares and comments by her old acquaintances had been enough to keep her away.

Mrs. Sawyer rounded the organ and came down the aisle, a fragile wren of a woman in bright purple slacks and a fuchsia top, with sturdy walking shoes on her delicate feet.

She pulled to a stop just a foot away from Tessa and looked up at her through thick trifocals. "Hi, dearie. I'll be done in a few minutes, if you've come to pray." Her eyes twinkled. "I know it must be distracting, with me thumping away on that organ." She leaned closer and lowered her voice to a whisper. "But after all these years, I've still got to practice, or I'll be in *real* trouble on Sunday mornings."

At once charmed and relieved, Tessa smiled in return. "Actually, I wonder if I could have just a couple minutes of your time."

The woman's face lit with pleasure. "Of course! We could sit in the babies' cry room at the back. The chairs are nice and comfy in there."

When they were settled in two of the padded rockers, Tessa pulled her list of names from her shirt pocket and handed it to Mrs. Sawyer. "I'm wondering about some people who lived around here. Do you know if they're still in the area?"

"Well, let me see." She bobbed her head until she zeroed in on the right part of her trifocals, then focused on the list and smiled. "Ahhh. Bill Clark—fine man. Far as I know, he's in Colorado. Ted Foster moved away years ago. Lowell Haskins is…away. His dad Harvey lives out at the old trailer park. Our Comfort and Care committee ladies tried bringing him food baskets, but he's a very proud and stubborn man."

So far, she hadn't been wrong on a single thing that Tessa knew already. "What about the Bassetts and the Irwins?"

Mrs. Sawyer frowned. "I'm pretty sure the elder Bassetts moved to Oklahoma. A couple of the young ones stayed…Lonnie and his brother Trace."

"Here in town?"

"They're ranch hands, I think, when they're not stirring up trouble. After their ranch went into foreclosure, that family never really recovered. I doubt they went on to college, but I don't know for a fact. Now, the Irwins are fine, upstanding folk. The mister runs the grocery store in Salt Grass, so they moved over there a while back. They both ought to be close to retirement by now." She studied the piece of paper. "Ahh, the Farleys," she said softly. "Now there was a sad case."

She darted a quick look at Tessa, faint color staining her weathered cheeks. "Oh, dear. I mean, sad because of Mr. Farley's health and all. They moved away, but I never heard where. They had the sweetest little ones—just like stair steps, they were. All red-heads like their momma."

Probably not the Irwins, then, of the final three. "If I wanted to talk to the Bassetts or the Farleys, would you have any idea where I should start looking?"

"The post office, maybe. Or the bank. Though these days, no one can say much of anything about anyone. So finding them won't be easy." She leaned forward and patted Tessa's leg. "But pray on it, because God does listen to all of your prayers."

Tessa's silent doubt must have shown on her face, because Mrs. Sawyer smiled. "His answers might not be what we expect, and some answers take longer to be answered—until exactly the right time. He loves His children, dearie. Trust in Him."

Tessa had the uncomfortable feeling that they were no longer talking about the Bassetts or the Farleys. But Mrs. Sawyer couldn't know about Tessa's past. No one in town did. She'd stayed at the ranch the entire nine months, and then there'd been a brief, graveside service at the family's private little cemetery up in the foothills.

But as she walked back to her truck, she felt an unexpected warmth unfurling in her heart.

Back at the ranch, Tessa did her barn chores, then went to her home office and started jotting notes about her trip to town.

Sofia appeared at the door a moment later, wiping her hands on her apron. "There's a fax for Josh coming through, so don't answer the phone if it rings. It's some lady magazine editor from New York."

"Editor?" Surprised, Tessa rocked back in her chair. Josh had mentioned some sort of photo assignment. Did that actually involve editors?

Sofia shrugged. "She said she tried to call his cell phone, but there was no answer."

"Probably because he's out of range."

"She asked about faxing something called a 'rough draft,' plus papers he needs to sign and send right back. I told her our fax number."

The phone started ringing, and after four rings the fax machine on the credenza kicked in. It sputtered and froze up for a second, then slowly chugged out three sheets of paper before jamming on the fourth.

Typical.

It was her third machine in less than a year, and so far the service contract she'd bought with the original unit was proving to be the best investment she'd made in ages. But that didn't help the fact that once something was partly delivered, it wasn't possible to hit a button and print it all over again.

"Good luck," Sofia said dryly. "That looks like a gonner to me."

And it was. Tessa gently tugged, tried opening the machine and pushing on the rollers, prying a letter opener between the gears, but ultimately, she was only able to retrieve a shredded, ink-smeared piece of paper.

She hesitated. "I hate to read any of this, but Josh won't be back for a couple hours. Maybe there's a letterhead with a phone number, so I could call her," she murmured. "What do you think?"

"You'd think they'd be closed by now, New York time. But maybe she's still near the machine and can re-send it, so Josh can take care of it first thing in the morning." Sofia backed out of the door and disappeared down the hallway. "I'll have supper ready at seven o'clock" she called out. "Then I need to go sit with Gus for awhile at the care center."

Tessa smiled, thinking about the long conversation she and Josh had enjoyed last night. He was still the only man who'd ever made her heart beat faster, and despite her earlier doubts, he was still a kind and thoughtful guy. Maybe he'd even decide to move out West someday…and then, who knew where *that* might lead, in time?

Tessa gingerly turned over the three intact fax papers, fixing her attention only at the top border.

Green Earth magazine.

And sure enough, a woman's name, address and phone number were listed under the company letterhead.

Tessa hesitated, feeling a flash of uneasiness at interfering. She started to dial, then stopped. The phone rang a minute later.

"Snow Canyon Ranch? Sylvia Meiers, here. I'm just checking to make sure my fax went through okay. Is Josh Bryant available?"

"He's out. This is Tessa McAllister."

"Ahh." The woman's voice filled with pleasure. "You're the young woman who has been helping him, right? He sent the article and photo files this afternoon, and I'll have to say, I think the article is dynamite."

Tessa forgot to breathe for a moment. *"Article?"*

"We've wanted to run a photo essay on the Wyoming Rockies situation for a long time, and your cooperation was invaluable."

Invaluable? "Um…the last page didn't come through."

"Ahhh…and that was the page he needs to sign. I'll send it again. You're welcome to read this draft of the article, by the way. He's a fine writer, and I think you'll be very pleased."

After hanging up, Tessa took a closer look at the documents in her hand, and the title said it all. *The Negative Impact of Grazing Rights on Public Land in Wyoming.*

Her heart sank as she forced herself to read the rest.

It had been a hot topic of debate for decades, sharply dividing local politicians, ranchers and environmentalists. And now Josh had sharply criticized the ranchers as carelessly destroying the priceless heritage of the land; the habitat of its native plants and animals.

And right below Josh's name was an acknowledgment of her assistance with researching the article.

A sick feeling worked its way through her stomach, tying it into knots. Josh had never said a word about anything beyond taking photographs. He'd promised to provide a fair and balanced view.

In all these weeks, there'd been *not one word* of anything more.

In the meantime, she'd been swept away, foolishly misled into believing that he truly cared for her, while she'd been falling in love with him in return. And he'd only been using her.

How could she have been so blind—the second time around?

"We did everything you said. *Everything.* Now where's the money?"

The person standing in the shadows met the man's glare with one of equal intensity. "You really didn't succeed now, did you? That ranch is still in business. She's alive and well. You've been thinking way too small."

"But—"

"You knew the deal before we started."

"I *ain't* risking the death penalty."

His business partner laughed, though it was an eerie, keening sound, without a trace of humor. "You won't. No one will ever figure it out, or have any idea that you were involved. And when it's all over, you'll have more cash in your pocket that you could possibly spend. Understood?"

The money. He'd lost sight of the reward, and all it could do. He relaxed, and smiled with satisfaction. "Understood."

EIGHTEEN

Josh unsaddled Jasper and turned him out into the pasture. Six months ago, the idea of spending seven hours in the saddle to count cattle and verify their good health was as far from his thoughts as flying to the moon. Yet here he was, dusty, tired, saddle sore, and he couldn't remember when he'd felt more fulfilled, or happier.

Though maybe that feeling had more to do with Tessa than a couple hundred head of cattle.

Which made his next task more daunting, more difficult than anything he'd done in a long while. When he got back to his cabin, he was going to pack, load up his motorcycle, and leave this ranch behind.

He wanted nothing more than to stay, but Tessa deserved better. A man worthy of her, who hadn't messed up his personal life over and over. A man who could truly love her without reservation. After Lara, he wasn't sure if he could ever fully commit to someone again. And how fair was that?

What had he ever done, but leave heartbreak in his wake?

* * *

"Y-you're leaving? Tonight?" Tessa glanced between the Harley and Josh. The lids on the big fiberglass saddlebags were open, filled to the brim with his clothes. His helmet was resting on the seat, on top of a red and black leather bomber jacket.

She'd been hurt and angry and ready for a confrontation when he returned this evening. She hadn't expected to find him packed and ready to go, without a word.

Then again, it shouldn't be a surprise.

He'd kept his reasons for being here a secret, and now his article was done. Why would he stay another minute? It didn't matter to him that its publication would do her irreparable harm. It didn't matter that she'd come to care for him once again.

She held out the faxes. "These came for you this afternoon. Your *editor* said she tried calling your cell phone, then looked up our ranch number on the Internet when you didn't return her calls. Imagine my surprise when she thanked me for helping you with your *article*—something I didn't even know existed, because you only admitted to taking photographs— and promised you would be providing a fair and honest view."

He hesitated for a split second, then accepted the documents without looking at them. "I don't blame you for being upset."

"'Upset' isn't quite the right word. Surprised. Betrayed. Used. Wait a minute—*devastated* works best. I'm not exactly sure how I 'helped' you, by the way. Did you just need a place to stay, or was it something more?" She threw her hands up in disgust. "Have you been ferreting out bits of information all along, to support your theories? Watching, and waiting to catch us doing something wrong?"

He flinched. "I always try to make local contacts who can help with information for an article, that's all. For *both* sides of the issue. But that wasn't how I ended up at your ranch."

"You just picked our place out of the blue?" she asked, incredulous.

"You rescued *me,* Tessa. Remember? You brought me home from the hospital."

"It seems mighty convenient that you *happened* to come to this precise part of the Rockies."

"Sylvia wanted me to do a photo essay on the effects of domestic animals on fragile government land." A faint smile touched his lips, though his eyes were filled with sadness. "I did decide on this part of the mountains because of you. You used to talk about the Wolf Creek area, and after doing some research, I figured it would be perfect. But I figured you'd graduated from college and gone on to a career. Even after I learned you had a business here, I thought you probably had someone else running it."

"Right."

"I never meant to hurt you, Tessa. This was my last

assignment, and I just wanted to get it done and be free of my contract—the sooner the better."

"Why?" The sudden shadows in his eyes made her wish she hadn't asked.

"I saw too much death. Our own soldiers. Innocent civilians. The…" He closed his eyes briefly. "The children. Suffering that never seemed to end. And for what? Did the losses make a difference—or weren't they just a needless tragedy?" He swallowed hard. "Then our own Humvee was hit, just days before we were to leave for the States—and Lara became one of those statistics. I tried to pull her free in time, but the whole vehicle exploded in a ball of flame. I…saw her die."

"Oh, Josh." Tessa fought the impulse to enfold him in a comforting embrace.

"I plan to donate the money from this Wyoming assignment to Lara's memorial, and then I'll leave that type of photojournalism behind. I just can't face covering any more violence, for a while, so now I'm considering a teaching position at a college in Boston. Though," he smiled, "after the motorcycle accident, and having a chance to spend time with you, I haven't been in a rush to go back east. But now, it's time."

"Well, it sure looks like you're in a hurry now." She glanced at his motorcycle, wondering how she could've ever imagined he might stay, then she stepped back. "By all means, don't let me stand in your way."

* * *

Tessa prowled through the house, unable to settle down with a book or a movie or the endless paperwork waiting on her desk. It was too early for bed. She knew sleep would elude her anyway.

A dozen thoughts started spinning through her brain in dizzying succession.

Where was Josh now? Had he made it to Rock Springs? Was he already on the interstate going east?

Mrs. Sawyer's comments on Tessa's list of suspects had matched what she'd discovered already. But of more interest was the fact that the Bassetts were still living in the area…and the uncomfortable reminder about the Farleys, who'd had four little redheads who were made homeless by Claire's greed.

There could be many other suspects, too, once Tessa had a chance to delve further into the past. But who could've been hurt badly enough to want retribution so many years later? And why had they waited this long?

And then she remembered the jeers of classmates when she was in third grade. The stiff greetings of shopkeepers in town, and the whispers that were always just loud enough for her to hear.

And the family photos in the bank that had inexplicably disappeared.

And suddenly it all made sense.

The lane out to the highway was a mile long; the longest mile of Josh's life.

It was right to leave.

It felt terribly wrong.

And only sheer strength of will kept him from turning back.

At the highway, he slipped off his helmet to adjust the strap and caught the acrid smell of smoke. Faint at first, then stronger, riding on the fitful wind.

He looked over his shoulder toward the ranch and saw it a quarter-mile back—the pulsing, threatening glow of fire speeding through the tinder-dry underbrush. It engulfed one pine tree after another, racing up the trunks and exploding, raining fire and ash, and sending flames in every direction.

And the wind was all wrong—heading straight for the ranch.

Tessa.

He made a sharp u-turn. Paused long enough to dial 911 on his cell phone. Then he roared back to the ranch and prayed every inch of the way.

NINETEEN

One minute, the deepening dusk was soft and quiet, save for the distant bawling of a mother cow. The next, the windows of the house reflected an eerie, orange glow sweeping across the horizon.

Fire.

Tessa jerked on her boots, grabbed her truck keys, and raced out onto the porch, cell phone in hand. A wall of fire glowed through the trees, menacing and powerful.

With a cry, she raced for the barn and opened the back door, then began opening the stall doors and chasing the horses out into the pasture. Smoke rolled down the aisle, sending them into a panic as they shoved past each other and escaped, whinnying and snorting.

Hobo and Elvis appeared out of nowhere, nipping at their heels and instinctively herding them along. When the last horse was freed, Tessa spun around and raced into the roiling smoke to the next building over, where there were four training horses. Her eyes were watering and her lungs were burning, burning, burning with every breath as she and the dogs drove those horses out into the pasture, too.

In the final building, she'd just made it halfway to the first stall when an odd sound made her turn around.

Her heart lodged in her throat at the sight of a tall, dark silhouette of a man standing in the doorway, backlit by the flickering orange and red sky.

And then another man joined him.

Shorter. Stocky. With a coil of rope held at his side.

"If it ain't Ms. McAllister," the taller one sneered.

The voice was deeper than she remembered. But she knew exactly who they were.

Trace and Lonnie Bassett.

"Please, help me. There's horses in here, and we've got to stop that fire!"

"Stop it? It's too late for that," Lonnie snickered. "That fancy house of yours will be cinders in no time, and these barns will be next. You ain't getting help anytime soon."

Horrified, she started backing up as they advanced on her, one slow step after another, as if they were stalking prey. "Y-you started the fire? *Why?*"

"It's business." Lonnie's voice was smug. "It's just a real shame that you had to be in the way."

Another fifteen feet back and she'd be up against the far door. Trapped without a weapon. And she could only imagine what they intended to do.

"W-we went to school together, remember? Same classes. And the senior prom—remember that? My date and I gave your truck a jumpstart." She scrambled desperately for any shared experiences she could think of—anything to personalize herself and make them pause. "And remember the rodeo—"

"Shut up! This ain't about you. It never was."

"But—"

Past their shoulders she caught a swift movement—someone crouched low and moving toward Lonnie and Trace, heading into the barn. Lonnie started to turn around.

She screamed to distract him as she darted to one side of the aisle and ducked into a feed room. She grabbed a gallon of fly spray and twisted off the wide lid, then held it down at her side, hidden behind her thigh. *It's not much, Lord, but please, please, make it work.*

She peered around the corner, and at that instant, Josh barreled into Trace's back, throwing him off balance. They crashed to the concrete floor in a tangle of arms and legs, with the sound of fists hitting flesh.

Lonnie hovered for a split second, then he turned to zero in on her, his eyes glittering and his breathing harsh. "Looks like it's me and you. This oughta be fun," he growled.

He closed the distance between them in four strides, the rope still in his hand. She could smell his breath, his sweat. He bared his teeth in a semblance of a smile—

With one swift movement she swung the gallon jug, spun, and sent the bitter, pungent liquid into his face.

He screamed, then sputtered and coughed, clawing at his eyes. Staggering blindly against the stall doors, he fell halfway to his knees with a guttural moan, then stumbled toward the barn door.

She turned to see Trace face down on the concrete floor, one arm wrenched up high behind his back as Josh knelt next to him.

"Tessa," he said. "Hurry—get me some baling twine."

She spun around and grabbed some twine from the feed room, then helped Josh securely bind Trace's hands behind his back.

They found Lonnie out at the water tank, scrubbing frantically at his face. Josh secured his wrists in front, so he could still splash water at the caustic residue.

Multiple sirens sounded in the distance, a nightmarish, discordant sound that promised help was on the way.

"I called 911 about the fire, so they should be sending a number of units in," Josh said. "There's not much we can do alone."

Towering flames shot into the sky as more pine trees were consumed. "Maybe you should stay with these guys, but that fire is getting too close," she cried. "Just an ember could burn the house down. I've got to do *something!*"

Grabbing a water hose from the barn, she ran for the hydrant at the side of the house closest to the flames, and started spraying the exterior walls and roof.

Acrid smoke billowed across the yard coupled

with waves of intense heat. But now, a half-dozen fire trucks and emergency vehicles were pulling in, plus several patrol cars.

And Tessa bowed her head in thanks.

Three days later, the smell of wet cinders still hung in the air, but luckily the firefighters had been able to contain the blaze to a little over fifty acres.

"Guess its time for me to go," Josh said, surveying the blackened landscape on the hillside above the barns and house. "Are you going to be all right?"

Tessa nodded. "I still can't believe Lonnie and Trace came after us like that. I know they've been in a lot of trouble over the years, but we've all known each other since school. How could they do that?"

"Greed. They were promised more money than Ellen Miller ever could've paid." Josh gave her a wry smile. "I suppose she figured they could hardly sue her for the difference."

"I can't imagine her dwelling on revenge for all these years. It must've poisoned everything else in her life."

"Michael said she was in fourth grade when Claire evicted her family from their rental house. The family ended up homeless for a long while, and then her parents split up. Since they hadn't lived in Wolf Creek for very long no one recognized Ellen when she moved back as an adult."

"So she was here, quietly waiting for her big chance—and she got it."

"She undoubtedly hoped you'd default on that loan, but she was also behind your other troubles at the ranch, according to Michael. She probably figured Trace was the perfect partner, because no one would look any farther than his own checkered past if he was ever caught. He and Lonnie have your missing cattle, by the way. They were planning to ship them later on, once people weren't watching for them any longer."

"Lonnie and Trace had their own reasons to see the McAllisters suffer," Tessa said sadly. "Not that it excuses what they did, but my mother had some sort of influence on the foreclosure of their ranch when they were kids."

"Which is probably why all three focused on your mother's ranch—and you because you run it. They wanted vengeance."

"What about the cabin burglaries? And Edward's death?"

"Michael thinks Trace has been breaking into cabins for a good year, and has been making quite a haul. A deputy found a big stash of stolen property at his place. His fingerprints matched those found at the murder scene, too. No word yet on a confession, but my guess is that Edward surprised him during a burglary, and Trace panicked."

"And Danny?"

"The judge has already released him."

Her heart lifted, despite the enormity of everything that had happened. "Thank goodness." She tried to swallow past the lump in her throat as she looked up at Josh. "You were wonderful, the night of the fire. I can't thank you enough for all you did."

"I'm just glad I came back in time." He climbed on his Harley and started the motor, regarding her with troubled eyes. "I…do owe you an apology about that magazine article. I finally read through it, and saw why you were so upset. The magazine used my photos with someone else's text, Tess. I guess mine didn't quite represent the magazine's world view."

"But your name was on that draft—and mine."

"I asked that they be removed." His wry smile reappeared. "The other writer gladly agreed."

"Thanks." She studied the gleaming chrome on his Harley to avoid meeting his eyes again. "That article would've put me in an awkward position with the other ranchers here, and it doesn't represent what I believe. But did you lose all the money, then?"

"Nope…and I've already sent it on to Lara's family, toward a memorial scholarship in her name. That's all I really cared about, not the byline."

She nodded, touched by his thoughtful gesture, but unable to find the words that would make things right. Knowing. With grim certainty, that he wouldn't have packed his things if he didn't want to finally escape Wyoming…and her.

"I won't forget you, Tess. I prayed so hard, when I saw you facing down Lonnie and Trace—I couldn't imagine this world without you in it…even if you and I are a continent apart."

She smiled sadly at that. "I was praying, too, believe me. But you really came through for me. If you hadn't been there—" She shuddered, trying not to imagine what could've happened.

"At least this time, I was able to make a difference." He sighed heavily, the expression in his eyes far away. "Second chance…different outcome. I'll always thank the Lord for that."

She looked up at him, wanting to wrap her arms around him and never let him go; realizing that such a gesture would just make this moment all the more awkward. "Thank you. For everything. I'll never forget what you did for me."

Their gazes met, locked for a long moment. Then he smiled in farewell and revved the engine before roaring down the lane in a cloud of dust.

Leaving her feeling…empty. Alone.

But, life would go on. Danny was back, and two new ranch hands would be starting next week. There would be pack trips, and chores, and all of the endless jobs at the ranch to keep her busy. She really wouldn't have time to miss him at all.

With a sigh, she headed for the tack room in the main barn. She stopped just inside the door…and blinked.

A saddle stand had been pulled into the center of the room. It held a blanket-covered saddle—probably one of the older ones that Danny was helping her restore.

But oddly enough, there was some sort of ribbon tied to the saddle horn, and an envelope lay on top of the blanket. Bemused, she moved closer and found her name on the envelope. She slid a finger under the flap and withdrew the handwritten letter.

Dear Tessa,

I know I've caused you a lot of pain over the years, and wish I could somehow make everything right.

This saddle doesn't begin to cover it all, but at least it might make you smile. I had a friend buy it online, so you wouldn't see my name as a bidder.

The sheriff recovered your saddle with the other stolen property in Trace Bassett's garage.

God Bless,

Josh

She gently lifted the blanket away, and there was her beautiful, custom made saddle—its silver polished and gleaming, the leather buffed.

Only now it wasn't just a beloved gift from Uncle Gray, but it would always be a link to Josh, who'd managed to steal her heart…twice.

She closed her eyes. In so many ways, she was a strong, take-charge woman, who let nothing stand in her way.

So why had she let him walk out of her life?

He'd left once before and made it just to the highway before turning back. This time, he wasn't stopping until he hit I-80 and was well on his way out East.

Miles. It would just take lots and lots of miles, and he'd be over Tessa McAllister for good. He wouldn't think about her smile, or her beautiful eyes, or her inner strength. He wouldn't think about how she made him feel, or the way he felt whole just being with her.

He wasn't going to think about her at all.

A half hour south of Wolf Creek, he started to slow down...just for safety.

An hour south, he started looking in his rearview mirror, as if he could catch a glimpse of her face.

After one more mile, he gave up. Turning around, he pushed the bike up to sixty-five.

Anything worth keeping was worth fighting for, and he was going to fight for Tessa. If it took years, he was going to prove to her that she could count on him, no matter what.

He hadn't seen another vehicle on this desolate highway in over an hour. Ahead, just a speck of dust on the horizon, he could see one now.

It drew closer.

His heart did a flip-flop in his chest when he realized it was a truck from Snow Canyon Ranch, and Tessa was behind the wheel.

They both pulled off to the side of the road in the middle of nowhere, surrounded by sagebrush and sand, with the jagged peaks of the Rockies off to the west.

"I made a mistake," she said simply. "I've spent too much of my life second-guessing decisions, analyzing things to death. Imagining that I'm in control. I'm finally realizing that maybe it isn't all about me.

Maybe it's time to take a leap of faith, and trust in God for what He has in store for us."

He cupped her face in his hands. "I love you, Tess. I think I always have, only it took nearly losing you to make me realize just how much. Before we mess this up one more time, I need to ask you—will you consider marrying me?"

She smiled and moved into his embrace, her head against his chest. "I love you, too, and believe me, you don't need to ask me twice."

EPILOGUE

The first blush of sunset cast the meadow in a rosy glow, as the wedding party gathered beneath a cathedral of towering pines. The Rockies, peaks still frosted with winter snows, soared skyward on the horizon.

From the edge of the meadow, where four surries and a number of saddle horses waited, came the sounds of jingling harnesses and soft whinnies. Children, impatient for the ceremony to begin, frolicked through the bowed grasses, picking bouquets of wildflowers. Off to the side, two members of the Wolf Creek Community Church played a violin and a portable Celtic harp, and the haunting, heart-breakingly perfect notes hung in the air, so beautiful and pure that Tessa felt her eyes burn.

Josh put his arm around her waist and drew her closer. "In October," he whispered, "it will be our turn."

"Can you imagine how lovely it will be, with all of the blazing fall colors out here?" She smiled up at him, her heart overflowing with love and joy.

Who would have thought, just a year ago, that life

would change so completely when she and her sisters came together to help their mother? Claire had always been a divisive force in the family, yet now her health had brought them back together in ways none of them could have predicted.

Tessa looked across the small crowd to where Janna and her husband stood talking to Pastor Lindsberg. Rylie and Ian, their blended family, were both excited about Janna's announcement last week—she and Michael would be welcoming a new little one in December.

Leigh—who had taken an emergency vet call this morning and who had just arrived at the meadow ten minutes ago, was now dressed in an ivory, antique Western-style wedding dress from the 1800s, with a matching, feather-trimmed hat and ivory lace-up boots. The wonder was that she didn't have a matching stethoscope draped around her neck, but she'd certainly found her perfect mate in Cole, whose new horse ranch was already prospering despite several setbacks. With their mutual interests and the obvious love they shared, Tessa had no doubt that their union would last forever.

Cole's young daughter Brianna was dressed like Rylie, in full-length, rose-colored lace bridesmaid dresses that matched those worn by Janna and Leigh, and watching the girls giggle and pirouette in their outfits made Tessa smile.

"Could there be a more perfect day?" she looked up at Josh and felt as if her heart could burst. "I don't think I've ever been happier. Look—even Claire seems to be enjoying this. Who would've guessed?"

Sure enough, Claire stood with Sofia and Gus at the far edge of the small meadow, near the rocky cliff that would serve as backdrop for the ceremony. And she was *smiling*...a rare expression that took years from her face.

When Josh just looked down at Tessa with compassion in his eyes, she knew what he was thinking, and it added a melancholy note to her joy. Claire had been increasingly forgetful lately. The doctor had warned the family that she could become more temperamental as her Alzheimer's progressed. But though she'd been irritating and demanding all her life, it was ironic that now—with her faculties fading—she was becoming more pleasant than anyone could ever remember.

Only those changes marked the grim progress of an enemy she couldn't defeat with her customary, hard-edged determination.

"Look!" Rylie shouted, pointing skyward. "Eagles!"

Three of them circled low overhead, soaring in intertwining circles, riding the thermals in a graceful ballet before finally disappearing over the treetops.

"That felt like a blessing," Tessa said, squeezing Josh's hand. "For all of us."

"Did you ever memorize that verse from Isaiah about eagles?"

She grinned, trying to pull the words together correctly. "But they who wait upon the Lord shall renew their strength; they shall mount up with wings as eagles; they shall run, and not be weary; they shall walk, and not faint."

"Good job!"

She tilted her head. "It was a favorite, when I was a kid, and I just looked it up this week. I've been thinking about my journey lately—I spent so many years angry at God about my pregnancy, and about losing the baby. I guess I wanted to make everything His fault. When really, I should have turned to my faith for strength and healing and comfort." She looked up at Josh with a rueful smile. "I would've been so much better off."

"I went through the same thing after Lara died. God was there, offering everything I needed to get through it all, but I turned my back on Him just when I needed him most. The one good thing was that it made me really look at my faith…and now I feel closer to Him than ever. It's given me a feeling of peace that I can't begin to describe."

The music faded. Then, after a heartbeat of silence, the pure, sweet notes of "Beautiful Savior" echoed through the clearing, sending shivers dancing across her skin—the perfect hymn for this glorious setting.

The crowd moved toward the chairs that had been set up facing the rocky altar. The pastor took his position in front of them, and behind the small congregation, Cole took Leigh's hand, ready for their walk down the aisle.

"I guess we'd better get over there—they can't

start without their wedding party," Tessa murmured. "Ready?"

"Not quite."

Their gazes met. Locked. And in his eyes, she saw everything she'd ever wanted. Love. Soul-deep acceptance. A relationship that would surely last until the end of time.

He kissed her gently, reverently, as if she were a fragile treasure, a kiss filled with the promise of everything that was to come.

And then they went to join the waiting crowd.

* * * * *

Dear Reader,

Welcome back to Wolf Creek, Wyoming, for the final story involving the McAllister sisters! I love the Wyoming Rockies and have really enjoyed writing about these strong, determined women, who each face challenges and unexpected dangers when they move back to help their aging mother.

Wildfire is Tessa's story. Growing up with a difficult, demanding mother shaped all three sisters, but Tessa's life has perhaps been the most challenging. She not only endured a devastating situation while in college, but has stayed on to help manage the family's Snow Canyon Ranch. With drought, the risky economics of ranching and a mother slipping into dementia, her life hasn't been easy.

I hope you'll enjoy Tessa's journey through dangers she can't predict, and the return of the one man she never, ever wanted to see again.

If you missed the first two books in the series, you can get them at www.SteepleHill.com. You can contact me through www.shoutlife.com/roxannerustand where you can also find information about book signings, upcoming book releases and free promotional items.

Wishing you blessings and peace,

Roxanne

QUESTIONS FOR DISCUSSION

1. Claire McAllister, a strong, determined rancher, was not a warm and nurturing mother to her three daughters, and this affected each of them in negative ways. Most parents want only the best for their children, but Claire was blind to her faults. Be it a friend or relative, is there any way someone could have helped her? Looking back, are there things that you wish had been different in your own childhood—or in how you raised your own children?

2. Tessa faced a traumatic incident during her first year in college—one that changed her life and badly damaged her faith, because she felt God had abandoned her. Have you ever struggled with your faith after something bad has happened? How could you help someone going through a situation like that?

3. Leigh and her sisters have been estranged for many years and are now working on breaking down those walls of misunderstanding. Can you ever fully repair a broken relationship? Why or why not?

4. Tessa felt a warm sense of peace when she finally stepped inside her childhood church again, after many years of feeling angry and hurt. Have you

developed a strong relationship with your church and its members? What can you do to strengthen those ties?

5. Tessa has alienated herself from God, but as the dangers mounted in this story, she started praying with increasing frequency, and eventually she returned to her church. Were her prayers answered? How often do you pray, and how has God answered?

6. Claire McAllister was showing signs of advancing dementia. Do you have a chronically ill person in your family, or know of another family who does? How does this challenge affect the family as a whole? Is the burden equally shared? Discuss ways in which family members can more effectively cope with this stress and how faith and prayer might help.

7. In one scene, Tessa worried that she might be turning out like her mother—with the ranch her only focus in life. How are you most like your own mother? Have you seen that change as you get older?

8. Tessa grew up with a strong, dominant mother, but without a father. What are the special challenges of being a single parent? What mistakes

did Claire make as a parent, and what might she have done differently to nurture her children in more positive ways?

9. Ellen Miller has held on to her anger at the McAllisters since childhood, and she has come back to town to seek vengeance. Perhaps she feels a twisted sense of satisfaction at exacting her revenge, but how might holding a grudge have affected her life and happiness all these years? Do you think she has led a full and abundant life in spite of her negative feelings? Can you think of any situations in which you have held on to your anger and hurt without being willing to forgive? What does the Lord's Prayer tell us about forgiveness?

10. Josh was overwhelmed when he learned about the birth and death of a son he never knew existed. Losing a child is terrible and heartbreaking. Have you or people close to you ever lost a child? Had a miscarriage or stillbirth? How can you best help a grieving parent?

11. Family relationships are a recurring theme in this Snow Canyon Ranch series. If Josh and Tessa had married as young college students, after she had found out she was pregnant, do you think their relationship would have succeeded? How might that have changed the people they are today?

12. The Bible verse quoted at the front of the book is Ephesians 2:2–5. How does that verse reflect Tessa's faith journey in this story? Do you think there's hope that Claire's heart will soften and that she'll eventually come back to Christ?

REQUEST YOUR FREE BOOKS!

2 FREE RIVETING INSPIRATIONAL NOVELS
PLUS 2 FREE MYSTERY GIFTS

Love Inspired
SUSPENSE

YES! Please send me 2 FREE Love Inspired® Suspense novels and my 2 FREE mystery gifts (gifts are worth about $10). After receiving them, if I don't wish to receive any more books, I can return the shipping statement marked "cancel". If I don't cancel, I will receive 4 brand-new novels every month and be billed just $4.24 per book in the U.S. or $4.74 per book in Canada, plus 25¢ shipping and handling per book and applicable taxes, if any*. That's a savings of over 20% off the cover price! I understand that accepting the 2 free books and gifts places me under no obligation to buy anything. I can always return a shipment and cancel at any time. Even if I never buy another book, the two free books and gifts are mine to keep forever.

123 IDN ERXX   323 IDN ERXM

Name	(PLEASE PRINT)	
Address		Apt. #
City	State/Prov.	Zip/Postal Code

Signature (if under 18, a parent or guardian must sign)

Order online at www.LoveInspiredSuspense.com

Or mail to Steeple Hill Reader Service:

IN U.S.A.: P.O. Box 1867, Buffalo, NY 14240-1867
IN CANADA: P.O. Box 609, Fort Erie, Ontario L2A 5X3

Not valid to current subscribers of Love Inspired Suspense books.

Want to try two free books from another series?
Call 1-800-873-8635 or visit www.morefreebooks.com

* Terms and prices subject to change without notice. N.Y. residents add applicable sales tax. Canadian residents will be charged applicable provincial taxes and GST. This offer is limited to one order per household. All orders subject to approval. Credit or debit balances in a customer's account(s) may be offset by any other outstanding balance owed by or to the customer. Please allow 4 to 6 weeks for delivery. Offer available while quantities last.

Your Privacy: Steeple Hill Books is committed to protecting your privacy. Our Privacy Policy is available online at www.SteepleHill.com or upon request from the Reader Service. From time to time we make our lists of customers available to reputable third parties who may have a product or service of interest to you. If you would prefer we not share your name and address, please check here. ☐

LISUS08

Love Inspired®
SUSPENSE

TITLES AVAILABLE NEXT MONTH

Don't miss these four stories in April

HIDDEN MOTIVE by Hannah Alexander

Sable Chamberlain's grandfather is dead, and an ice storm has her trapped with all the suspects. If Sable and her coworker, Paul Murphy, can't solve the murder in time, they won't be able to protect themselves from being next on the hit list....

IN HIS SIGHTS by Carol Steward

Reunion Revelations

Despite the two suspicious deaths pushing Magnolia College into the limelight, publicist Dee Owens is determined to restore her alma mater's reputation. And now, thanks to Dee's expert damage control, all eyes are on her—including the murderer's.

LAKEVIEW PROTECTOR by Shirlee McCoy

A LAKEVIEW novel

When Jasmine Hart loses her family, her life shuts down... until Sarah, her mother-in-law, asks for her help. Ex-military man Eli Jennings is in town as a favor for a friend, but when Sarah disappears, Jasmine and Eli must work together to find her—and unravel the secret she's been keeping.

WITNESS by Susan Page Davis

There's no body and no evidence, but Petra Wilson still claims she saw her neighbor strangle his wife. No one believes her, except for private investigator Joe Tarleton...and the killer, who is determined to silence the only witness.

LISCNM0308